TYNE E. TELLS

TANYA F. MARION

D1075590

Copyright © 2019 by Tanya F. Marion
Illustrations by Jeremy Sutherland
Cover design and interior layout by Anurup Ghosh

First edition 2019
ISBN 978-1-7333786-0-4

This book was typeset in 12 pt. Palatino.
Published by WriteSpike Inc.

For Savvy

You are the greatest story I will ever tell.

I love you more.

Mom

Chapter One

Granddad's Story

I really don't know what made me want to climb

into the attic that Sunday night when I first discovered

the trunk. I'd never been up there by myself. I never

really had a reason to before that night. I had always

gone up there with my mom, usually in December to

unpack the Christmas decorations, or in January to

repack the Christmas decorations. But this was May.

Christmas had long passed and wasn't due to arrive

again anytime soon. However, that night the trunk in the

attic called to me like Christmas morning.

There was nothing especially noteworthy about it, besides the manila envelope that had been taped to the top and the unexplainable fact that I had never, in all my twelve years, seen the trunk in the attic until that night. The brass-wrapped edges were badly tarnished, and the hinges were so rusted that replacement hinges off a pirate's sunken treasure chest would have been an improvement.

Inside the manila envelope were loose, typewritten pages accompanied by a short, handwritten note:

My Sweet Savvy,

> *My messenger is small, so my words must be few. He'll bring them each night, but only to you.*

> *You are my heart,*

> *Granddad*

He'd been gone for nearly a year, but those words rang in my ears as if he were there speaking them himself.

Attempting to sort the many thoughts shooting through my mind at warp speed, I managed to muster, "Granddad?" in a voice so faint a mouse would have to cup a paw behind his ear to hear it.

Who would have known the story on those pages would change my life forever? Certainly not me. And even now, I still wonder. I wonder if this was all part of Granddad's plan. I wonder if the book ended the way he'd hoped.

My granddad started my story, and he started it with the loose typewritten pages I found in the attic that uncommon Sunday night. When I found them, I did just as you are about to do now. I lifted the pages close to my face and began to read…

The Story of the Coat of Tyne E. Tells

Whumpf! Whumpf! Whumpf! Tyne E. kept swinging at Robert until Ms. Gibbs ran across the

schoolyard and broke up the scuffle. She hadn't seen
Robert throw the first blow or the way he'd made fun of
Tyne E. before the fight began. Robert Newmouse was
known for causing trouble, and this was no exception. It
had all started earlier that day when Tyne E. got on the
bus.

"You can sit with me."

Looking up and down the bus for a seat, Tyne E.
paused for a moment to make sure the voice he'd heard
was talking to him. When he turned around, there she
was, Dottie MaeMouse. Dottie was the loveliest, kindest,
smartest, most popular, and most beautiful mouse in the
whole school. And in Tyne E.'s eyes, she was perfect. Her
fur was white with a slight hint of grey, like a movie
screen when nothing is playing on it. Her eyes were a
shade all their own. They were too dark to be called
purple, too vibrant to be called black, and too clear to be
called grey. But no matter the color of Dottie Mae's eyes,

Tyne E. could hardly glance at them without losing his wits.

"I'll move my backpack," said Dottie as she lifted it from beside her and tucked it between her left foot and the bottom of the seat in front of her.

"Um, okay. Th, thanks." Tyne E. felt his cheeks turn hot and his throat begin to close. An awkward grin spread across his face from whisker to whisker.

"You almost missed it," said Dottie.

"Uh?" Tyne E. managed to mutter. He'd hoped the words, "missed what?" would follow, but they never did. Sitting beside the prettiest mouse in school had made him nearly speechless.

"The bus. You almost missed the bus," clarified Dottie with raised brows. The corners of her mouth curled ever so slightly upward, making Tyne E. all the more shy.

"Um, yeah, I, I kind of overslept," Tyne E. replied awkwardly.

As the bus rolled away, Tyne E. timidly settled into the seat beside Dottie, shuffling his backpack from his lap to the floor.

"You dropped your coat," said Dottie with a kind nod and an outstretched pointing paw. Tyne E. glanced downward and saw his coat lying in the aisle of the bus.

"Oh yeah, thanks," he replied, finally mustering a string of words with a slight hint of confidence. Tyne E. leaned over to pick up his coat, but just as he did, a foot briskly sent the coat airborne.

"Hey!" yelled Tyne E. "Watch it, that's my coat." The coat landed halfway down the length of the bus and was promptly followed by none other than Robert Newmouse. Robert picked up the coat and yelled back down the aisle toward Tyne E.

"Coat!" he mocked. "This isn't a coat; it belongs in a trash can. And when we get to school, that's where it's going!"

"Give me my coat!" Just as Tyne E. leapt from his seat to grab the coat, the words, "STAY IN YOUR SEATS," reverberated throughout the bus after they were bellowed from a large figure sitting behind the wheel.

Tyne E. plopped himself down, redirecting all the force he had just planned to use on Robert Newmouse toward the seat beneath him.

"You can get it back when we get to school," said Dottie. "Don't pay any attention to Robert."

Tyne E. stewed in silence the entire ride. He sat next to Dottie in total, complete, utter embarrassment. The wheels could not roll fast enough. When the bus stopped at the school, Tyne E. got off before Robert Newmouse and waited to confront him.

"Give me my coat, Robert," demanded Tyne E. "Where is it?" With at least half a dozen teachers looking on, Tyne E. persisted with the grilling, but his coat was nowhere in sight. Robert had stuffed Tyne E.'s coat in his book bag, and wasn't about to take it out and admit his guilt in front of everyone; he was too smart for that.

"Give me my coat! I know you have it!" yelled Tyne E. as he reached for Robert's bag. Knowing their homeroom teacher, Ms. Gibbs, was watching, Robert played the role of innocence well enough to win an Oscar.

"Let go!" shouted Robert. "Let go of me! Get your paws off me, Tyne E.! Get off!"

"Tyne E.," scolded Ms. Gibbs, "to the principal's office right now!"

"But Ms. Gibbs, he has my…"

Whumpf! As soon as Ms. Gibbs turned her head, Robert sucker punched Tyne E. right in the soft part of his stomach, and when he did, Tyne E. charged headfirst into the school bully. Only half Robert's size, Tyne E. was a scrapper. He'd grown up with two older brothers, so he knew how to fight. Thud! The two mice hit the ground, and Ms. Gibbs turned to see Tyne E. on top of Robert with his fist pulled back like a loaded sling shot.

Whumpf! Whumpf! Whumpf!

"Tyne E.!" hollered Ms. Gibbs frantically. "Stop!" She ran toward the two mice, reaching them just in time to stop Tyne E. from releasing his last sling shot punch.

Robert and Tyne E. spent the rest of the day sitting in detention where they exchanged sneering glances and muffled remarks.

That afternoon, after hearing Tyne E.'s side of the story, Ms. Gibbs checked Robert's bookbag. She pulled out a coat covered in dirt smears and loosely hanging, ripped threads. "Is this yours, Tyne E.?"

Not even needing to look up, Tyne E. took the coat, wadded it in a ball, and stuffed it under his arm. If it hadn't looked like a hand-me-down mess of fabric before, it certainly did now.

Exhausted and still angry, Tyne E. walked home that afternoon, threw his tattered coat in the trash, and went straight to his room.

He'll never let that go, thought Tyne E. as he plopped across his hay bed. He knew that wasn't the last time he'd have to deal with Robert Newmouse. He had stood up to Robert, yes, but he'd done it in front of the whole school. *He'll never let that go.*

With that thought, Tyne E. slipped into a world less cluttered by reality and more ruled by dreams of what could be. He slept peacefully, forgetting the fight with Robert Newmouse, envisioning only things to come – marvelous things, wonderful things, impossible things. Echoing between his dreaming ears, reverberating even louder than his snores, Tyne E. heard the sound of the ground trembling. He was winning the race. Gallop after gallop he rode to the finish line, paces ahead of every other contender.

You see, Savvy, what I haven't told you is that Tyne E. had a destiny. Not even Tyne E. knew what awaited him. It was a destiny so big and so unlikely that you may not even believe me when I reveal it to you.

But Tyne E. wasn't ready. Sure, he was fearless, full of grit and determination, but he didn't know how to use it. And his destiny depended upon him learning.

Chapter Two

The First Set of
Pages Continued

A Thread of Confidence

When Tyne E. awoke the next morning, the first thing he did was check the clock that ticked dependably on the nightstand beside his bed. *Six forty-five*, thought Tyne E., *I've got a few more minutes.*

"Rise and shine," bellowed Mrs. Tells as she entered Tyne E.'s room with the force of an invading army. "Pancakes are ready, syrup and peanut butter are on the table, milk is poured, let's go! Up, up, up!"

"Mom! Go away! I'm up! Pleeease just go!"

"Okay," whispered Mrs. Tells in retreat. "I just wanted to make sure you got a better start to today than you did yesterday. Breakfast is waiting, along with a little surprise. It's draped over your chair. I would ask who it belongs to, but it seems to already have your name on it," she said with a self-satisfied grin and closed the door. Tyne E. opened his eyes a little wider and began to rub his face while still lying comfortably on his hay bed. As the fog of sleepiness receded, he remembered his coat.

Mrs. Gibbs had called Tyne E.'s mom the night before and told her everything that had happened.

Figuring that his mom had likely found the coat in the trash and wondering what surprise she had draped over his breakfast chair, Tyne E. leapt from his bed. He dressed himself quickly, fumbling the buttons on his light blue, oxford cloth shirt. His paws were moving at a quickened pace that couldn't keep time with his anxious and excited imagination. His mom had changed his coat in some way; that much he knew for sure. But whether or not he would like it, well, that was still to be discovered. With a quick swipe of the brush, Tyne E. combed his fur. *Swipe, swipe, swipe, swish, gargle, swish, gargle*; Tyne E. finished brushing his teeth. After an, "Ahhh," and a satisfied smile at his reflection, Tyne E. paraded down the stairs in perfect cadence. *Ba dum, badum, badum.* He intentionally hid his excitement by sporting an air of coolness.

When Tyne E. reached the kitchen and saw his coat for the first time, that air of coolness faded. His mom, a master seamstress, had transformed it. The coat was spectacular.

"I spent most of the night on it," commented Mrs. Tells lovingly.

Tyne E.'s eyes perused the detailing on the coat. Mrs. Tells had covered a melted bubble gum stain, which had long ago found its home on the front pocket of Tyne E.'s coat, with a personalized patch complete with Tyne

E.'s initials. On the opposite pocket, she had designed a family crest patch with a deep garnet background, inlaid with golden thread. The name *TELLS* was proudly displayed on the patch like a royal title. She had repaired all of the small tears and trimmed every piece of frayed fabric. She had replaced every clear plastic button with a shiny, ornate brass button topped with an engraved *T*, and had reinforced each buttonhole with the same deep garnet thread that she'd used to make the background of the family crest patch. Finally, she had lined the inside of the coat with a soft, golden mulberry silk so that it felt as comfortable and welcoming as a favorite blanket.

"Mom, I don't know what to say. This doesn't even look like the same coat."

"Do you like it?"

Tyne E. slid his arms into the silk-lined sleeves. He popped the collar of his new coat and grinned. "I love it."

"Well, the fit couldn't be better. I let the sleeves out a bit to give you growing room. And I..." Mrs. Tells stopped herself abruptly. She almost told Tyne E. about the special message she had sewn inside the cuff of his sleeve, but decided to wait. Her motherly instincts told her there might be a better time, and when Tyne E. needed the message the most, he would find it.

"And what, Mom?" asked Tyne E. as he poured warm maple syrup over a melted layer of peanut butter that covered a stack of pancakes so large it looked like an iced layer cake.

"Pancakes again!" interrupted Tall, Tyne E.'s oldest brother, as he scurried through the kitchen with precision and purpose. "Mom, you know they are full of carbs and simple sugars. We just did a project on this in biology. I got an A of course. Just ask me, I can tell you all you need to know about dietary health."

"And about everything else." Tyne E. chuckled, mocking his older brother. Tall was smart, probably the smartest of the three brothers, and he enjoyed showing it. He always had an answer for everything and plenty of advice for his younger brothers whether they liked it or not.

Tyne E. smacked his syrup-covered lips and gulped his milk while Tall briskly prepared his own special breakfast.

"Bread made of whole sprouted grains, organic of course, topped with thinly sliced carrots and perfectly ripened avocados. Bon appetit! Want some?" asked Tall as he pushed his plate across the table toward Tyne E.

Swoosh, crunch, "Blah!" No sooner could Tyne E. decline Tall's offer, than his other brother Harry scurried by grabbing the sandwich and tasting it upon immediate regret. "Ugh, this is awful! Be glad I saved you from this, little brother," said Harry as he tossed the sandwich back onto Tall's plate.

"Great. Now I'll have to make another one," grumbled Tall.

"It's fine. I only took a bite."

"No," replied Tall, "it has fur gel on it!"

Harry stopped piling pancakes onto the plate his mom had handed him and looked at the sandwich. Of the three brothers, Harry was an icon of style. His clothes were pristine at all times, and only the most current trends were allowed to adorn his closet shelves. Independent and proud, he bought all of his clothes himself. He had an entrepreneurial spirit and would make extra money by braiding and styling his friends' fur. All of the girl mice loved him, and he became most popular right before any big dance. Every mouse in school wanted their fur styled by Harry.

"Oh, you're right." Harry grimaced. "I wouldn't eat that if I were you." Harry wiped the extra fur gel from the top of his paw, and proceeded to devour his own stack of melted-peanut-buttery, maple deliciousness.

"I've got to get ready for work, boys," announced Mrs. Tells. "Your father and I have a big install today. The new family in barn *Sixteen* has ordered curtains for their renovated two-story burrow. They had your father build seventeen windows in that burrow. Seventeen! That's the biggest order Building Tells has had in the company's whole existence, and I have to install the curtains on all seventeen windows today! Have a great day at school, and look out for your little brother!" Mrs. Tells disappeared from the kitchen into the hallway.

"Let's take a look at this," said Harry as he lifted Tyne E.'s coat from the back of his chair. "This doesn't look like the coat Mom found in the trash yesterday."

"Give it back, Harry!" Tyne E. reached for the coat unsuccessfully.

"Okay, okay, don't be so sensitive. I only wanted to take a look." Harry handed the coat back. Tyne E. grabbed the coat and buried it in his lap, safely stashing it between the tops of his furry thighs and the underside of the splintery, wooden breakfast table.

"You know, Tyne E., Mom told us what happened with Robert Newmouse, and I'm pretty sure I could help," Tall said.

"I don't need help."

"Sure you do." Tall insisted. "I can represent you. Just tell me all the facts of the case, and I'll pay a visit to Robert Newmouse to discuss peaceable reconciliation."

With his furry right brow raised in doubt of the effectiveness of Tall's proposal, Harry interjected, "You've heard the saying kill 'em with kindness? Well I say win 'em with blindness, and by that I mean blind him with beauty! Let me do your fur. I've been developing a new furdo. I call it *The Mouselet*. First, we spike your top furs, then we feather the sides, and to perfect the look, we grow out the back."

"Thanks guys, but I'm going to handle this my way," replied Tyne E.

"What are you going to do?" asked Tall and Harry in surprisingly perfect unison, as if their concern for their brother had momentarily joined the two mice in a rare occurrence of solidarity.

"I'm going to do the only thing I can do: I'm going to outsmart him."

When Tyne E. left for school that morning, he felt ready. Unlike the day before, he'd got up on time, his clothes matched, his teeth were brushed, his fur was combed, and his coat looked splendidly spruce. He climbed the steps of the bus and looked up in hopes of finding Dottie with a free seat beside her. There she was, a few rows back. Dottie sat with her head tilted downward and her eyes perusing her history notes. Without awaiting an invitation, Tyne E. scampered toward Dottie's seat and sat down next to her.

"Oh hey," she said, looking up from her notes and smiling. "I didn't even realize we were at your stop. I've got this huge quiz second period. I think I'm ready." She tucked the loose pages of notes into her backpack. "Is that new?" Dottie touched Tyne E.'s coat sleeve.

"Oh this?" Tyne E. replied while lifting the lapel of his coat. "You could say that."

"It's nice," said Dottie with a warm grin. "I hope you didn't get in too much trouble yesterday."

"No, why? Oh, you mean the thing with Robert. No, I'm not worried about that." Tyne E. tried to collect every morsel of confidence he could because he knew whose stop was next. The bus rolled to a screeching halt as the thinning brake pads announced their need for replacement. Normally, the sound would send an autonomic cringe throughout Tyne E.'s body, but this time was different. This time Tyne E. could have listened to the sound as if it were music, as long as it meant more time with Dottie by his side and less time with Robert Newmouse, whose figure was placing a shadow against the steps of the bus foretelling his entrance.

Robert looked at Tyne E. and sneered. "Well, well."

"To your seat!" The bus driver pointed down the aisle. He meant business. "I'll not have a repeat of yesterday, boys."

"I'm not doing anything," Robert said. His voice dropped to a whisper. "At least not yet." A wry smile spread across his devious, ill-proportioned face.

Tyne E. remained stoic. His posture and expression were fixed in a calm display of sureness.

Dottie affectionately nudged Tyne E. with her elbow and spoke softly, "That went okay."

The rest of the ride consisted of quick, endearing glances and poorly-timed awkward laughs, but for Tyne E., it was heaven. Tyne E. spoke more to Dottie on that one short ride to school than he had the entire year. By the time they reached the school, Tyne E. was so spellbound that you could nearly see the fur on his chest rise and fall with each beat of his heart. The bus pulled to a stop, and everyone made their way to the front, bumping one another with swaying backpacks as they tussled their way to the exit. Tyne E. looked up to see Robert just two mice behind him. He knew he needed to move quickly so as to not get trapped in his seat with Robert on one side of him and Dottie on the other.

"Come on." Tyne E. stepped in front of the next mouse and made a space for Dottie to join in line. He took her bag with his right paw and grazed the back of her shirt with his left as he let her take the spot in front of him. For a moment, Tyne E.'s world was perfect. He didn't care that Robert loomed just two mice behind him. All he saw was who stood before him. When they reached the front of the bus, a chilly breeze burst through the doorway with fierce purpose. It seemed to have missed every mouse before them and every mouse behind them. Dottie shivered and, without any hesitation, Tyne E. reacted. With supreme confidence and assuredness, Tyne E. dropped his shoulders letting the silky lining of his coat glide smoothly down his arms. He caught the collar of his falling coat in his paw and, with a swift lift, wrapped the coat around Dottie's shoulders.

The coat cascaded over her petite mousy figure as if it were designed with her custom measurements in mind.

Robert was in mid-sentence, taunting Tyne E. from behind, when he saw Dottie wearing the coat. He stopped. What was he going to say now? Tyne E. had somehow managed to convince the prettiest, most popular girl in school to wear his old coat. And to make Tyne E.'s quiet victory all the more definitive, the coat Dottie sported around school that day displayed the name TELLS eliminating all doubt as to whom it belonged. From that day forward, Tyne E.'s place in the hierarchy of school social status was forever changed. In a moment of confrontation, Tyne E. showed courage and kindness, and that meant more than any words Robert Newmouse could have ever said.

That's when I knew Tyne E. was destined for something grand. He was no ordinary mouse nor did he act in ordinary ways. That day on the bus taught him that every situation had a solution, and what seems like a great problem today can turn into a great opportunity tomorrow. For you see, Savvy, as I said before, Tyne E. Tells had an extraordinary destiny ahead of him, and now he was one step closer to fulfilling it.

And with those words, I'd read the last of the first set of pages my granddad had sent to me. When I finished reading the typewritten pages, I picked up the handwritten note and read it again, aloud this time:

My messenger is small, so my words must be few. He'll bring them each night but only to you.

# Chapter Three

I'd Rather Not Say

The morning after discovering the trunk was much like any other. Mom and I both rushed our way through the A.M. routine with expert precision. We had a way of maneuvering around our small kitchen that bore semblance to stealthy commandos on a time sensitive mission. We never got in one another's way. I guess that was because it had just been the two of us for as long as I could remember.

"Did you get enough sleep last night, hun?" asked my mom, breaking the morning silence. I was never a morning person. I'm still not. My mind felt cloudy as if my head were filled with fizzy soda sloshing my brain around like a dinghy in a storm.

I managed to audibly form the words "Umm, I guess so," through a yawn so intense that my jaw ached a little after it had passed. "Mom, I found a trunk in the attic last night." Mom stopped slicing the strawberries she had planned to top our toasted waffles with and looked over her shoulder at me.

"You found it." Her gazed shifted downward as her shoulders fell slightly forward. Time seemed to slow as Mom stood there with her back to me. If not for the sound she made, as if she was trying to swallow an uncomfortably large lump in her throat, I might have thought she'd turned into a statue. I waited patiently. She finally raised her head, turned around, gave a forced smile, and explained, "It was Granddad's. He wanted me to keep it for you until your thirteenth birthday."

"So he gave it to you before he…" I paused. I couldn't seem to say the words. The sadness was still too fresh on my heart.

"Yes, sweetie." Mom walked over to me and put her hands on my shoulders. She had a small piece of strawberry stuck to the callous on the side of her middle finger. "He loved you so much, Savannah. And I know you miss him. I miss him, too." She hugged me as only a mom could, with the magic type of hug, the type that seems to make everything a bit better. "Did you open it? The note on the top, I mean. He made me promise not to read it before I gave it to you."

I was a little hesitant to tell Mom what the note had said. After all, it wasn't the standard *Happy Birthday* written on a four-dollar celebratory card. I wanted to keep the words of Granddad's note to myself, at least until I figured out exactly what it was they meant.

"Yes," I replied hesitantly. My mom raised her brows and tilted her head forward as if awaiting more detail. "He, um, he told me he loved me and that I was his heart." Sure, it was a divergence from the whole truth but at least omission wasn't outright lying.

Mom's brow fell back to its usual position. Then she smiled and softly said, "Sounds just like him." For a moment, everything felt as it had before. The fizz in my mind had flattened. The storm in my head had calmed, and the dinghy that was sloshing about only moments ago had found itself beached on the serene island of past memories. I could only remember the good times. I think that's how it works. You remember the best and the rest seems to float away.

"Oh no, I've stained your shirt," Mom said, interrupting my serene moment, after spotting the stowaway bit of fruit that had hitched a ride from her finger to my shirt. "I'm sorry, sweetie. Go put on a fresh shirt, okay? We only have five minutes before we need to leave."

The ride to school that morning seemed shorter than normal, and the surprise that awaited me fifth period was approaching quickly. Had I known what was in store for me, I might have told my mom to hit the brakes and let me out of the car. When we passed the fork in the road at the old bait and tackle store, I knew we only had five minutes left on our drive. That old store was my mile marker because every now and then, Mom would stop there and buy us each a box of donut holes. They sold the best donut holes. Sugary, glaze-encased spheres of warm, perfectly baked dough filled our car with the most mouthwatering smell whenever we stopped there. But this morning there had been no time for sweet detours. Before I knew it, I'd arrived with only moments to spare, and the countdown to fifth period Biology, the class that started this best-selling author adventure I've been on for the past year, had begun.

As soon as I walked through the front door of my school, I heard the homeroom bell reverberate through the halls like a shrill scream. Everyone hated that bell. It was electronic and for the past month had developed a high-pitched glitch.

"Savannah Ashford."

"Here, Ms. Borellis," I said while rushing to my seat.

"You're lucky I called roll in reverse this morning, Ms. Ashford," said Ms. Borellis with a smile. Try to be a little earlier tomorrow." Ms. Borellis was always a kind teacher. She taught English and creative writing and had been my homeroom teacher for two years in a row.

"They still haven't fixed that bell. I'm pretty sure we'll all have hearing loss by the time we reach high school," whispered Kristen chuckling from the seat in front of me.

"Everyone please stand for the Pledge," requested Ms. Borellis. While certain members of the class respectfully pledged allegiance to the flag, a few inanely recited their own versions, something Ms. Borellis dearly hated but always chose to ignore.

"Lunch today will be chicken fingers, rice with gravy, green beans, cornbread, and fruit cocktail for dessert. I need a show of hands for those who want lunch

from the cafeteria. One, two, three, four, five, six, seven…"
counted Ms. Borellis.

"Psst," I poked the back of Kristen's arm. "I saw
something last night in our attic."

"That sounds frightening."

"No, I don't mean like that. I mean I found
something." *BRIIIIIII!* "Ugh, that bell. You're right!"

"What?" asked Kristen with one finger pressing
against her right ear. *IIIIIIING.*

"About the hearing loss," I replied.

"Oh!" Kristen laughed. "Yeah, I think it's already
started," she said while hoisting her backpack over her
shoulder in preparation to leave for first period.

"Oh, I'd better warn you. We're having a pop quiz
in English today. Ms. Borellis told us before you got here,"
said Kristen.

"Great. I didn't study at all last night. Thanks for
the heads up!"

"Hey, tell me about the attic thing at lunch. Okay?"

"Yeah." I nodded, and the countdown to fifth period biology continued – homeroom down, four classes to go.

Kristen and I had been friends since third grade, and this was the first year we didn't have all the same classes. She had gym first period, and I had Math Misery 101. For me, plus signs, subtraction signs, multiplication signs, and any other scribbled figures denoting mathematical instruction, might as well have been Mandarin Chinese. Actually, I'm quite certain Mandarin would have been easier, but for Mr. Aslo, mathematics was his native tongue. He soared through calculation after calculation marking the chalkboard with short abrupt strikes of colored chalk. Even the way he formed his numbers looked intense. It was as if his eights, nines, and sixes all had squinting, beady eyes that followed me no matter where I sat in the room. This year, I was assigned a seat in the front row, and the eyes had been especially keen. At the end of first period, I threw my backpack over my shoulder and headed to my next class. Only three more classes stood between me and my fifth period surprise.

Second period was nothing like Mr. Aslo's class. If school were a cookie, Ms. Watts' second period history was the chocolate chips. Mr. Aslo's math was the pinch of salt. History was the class I could slide through with very little effort. It was the class where I could do things like study for my upcoming pop quiz in English while still retaining enough of Ms. Watts' lectures to make an A at the end of the quarter. And I wasn't the only one. Most days a good portion of the class passed around notes when Ms. Watts wasn't looking. I sat in the back, so I got to see everything, like when Billy Marshall put ten paper spit balls in Tracy Snyder's hair while she sat in front of him intently copying the bullet points Ms. Watts was writing on the board. What Billy Marshall didn't know was that each time he reached forward to place a new paper spit ball in Tracy's hair, Tracy's best friend Ryleigh

McBride, who sat behind Billy, would put two paper spit balls in Billy's hair. The whole day Billy Marshall walked around a marked example of Ryleigh's paper justice. No one ever told him that his hair was sprinkled with remnants of one of Ryleigh McBride's notebook pages. It wasn't until fourth period when Billy woke up from sleeping on his desk and reached to scratch his head that he noticed the small, round bits of karma scattered throughout his sandy brown hair.

After coasting through second period, fifth period was drawing even closer. There were only two more classes before my world would change because of an assignment I wasn't expecting. Once again, I hoisted an even heavier backpack, and trekked my way to third period.

Third period was English with Ms. Borellis again, and as much as I liked her, I always counted the passing minutes during her class with famished anticipation. It never failed that no matter what I ate for breakfast, it didn't stick with me long enough to make it through the end of English without my stomach embarrassingly announcing to everyone that it had needs, and its needs superseded the art of sentence diagramming or the rote recitation of Ms. Borellis' twenty comma rules.

When lunch finally arrived, it was a welcome break and meant that I could catch up on all the school gossip with Kristen while I hushed the embarrassing alarm my stomach had set on midday repeat. In hindsight, had I known what was in store for me in fifth period, we would have had even more to talk about that day.

After lunch was fourth period Computer Science. It was the flour in the school cookie, necessary but unpalatable. Also taught by Mr. Aslo, number-wielding extraordinaire, it was no surprise that I'd take a slight pause everyday before entering the room. I'm still not sure if the pause was due to a nervous twitch brought on by a mental repellant of anything relating to numbers –

even if it was just ones and twos – or if it was more spiritual: time spent in short prayer to pass the class with at least a C but preferably a B minus.

Finally, *finally*, fifth period arrived. I couldn't have known what was about to happen: that a Biology project was going to cause such a stir at Ward Middle, or that by the end of the week, everybody in my class would be counting on me to save their grades. But that's exactly the chain of events I sparked when I walked into Biology class that Monday afternoon.

"Everyone take a seat," instructed Mr. Weiss. Biology was the sugar in the school cookie, and other than English, was the only class I shared with Kristen. We sat near the back, beside the model skeleton and beneath a poster of the anatomy of the human eye that had been hanging by only three corners for the past two weeks. The poster had bothered me every day I'd seen it hanging askew, but that day I barely noticed it thanks to the reflection of light bouncing from a silver-toned, metal pan on my desk that begged for my attention. Every desk in the room had the same metal pan and silver-toned tools sitting atop it. Some of the tools I recognized, like the scissors and the magnifying glass, but others looked strange to me.

"Today, we are going to learn about the art of dissection," announced Mr. Weiss.

Dissection, I thought. Unless we were going to be cutting up last quarter's report card, dissection was of no interest to me. So far this year, biology had been a fun class and one that I'd really enjoyed. We did cool experiments and watched fun videos about how to do more cool experiments. But like I said, biology class was like the sugar in the school cookie. It's fun at first. However, you have to stop before you reach the point of getting a stomachache, and I had a feeling we were about to reach that point.

"What you each have on your desks is a collection of basic dissecting equipment. You will find a dissecting pan, a hand lens, a scalpel, forceps, scissors, probes, a metric ruler, and T-pins."

Billy raised his hand. "Um, Mr. Weiss?"

"Yes, Billy."

"Are we really going to dissect something? I mean like an animal or something?"

"Yes, Billy," replied Mr. Weiss. "We really are going to dissect an animal."

"Gross!" squealed the gaggle of four cheerleaders who always sat together in the back of the room. I looked over my shoulder at Kristen who sat just behind me and to the left. Kristen knew me like a sister. I'd always wanted a sister, and she was the closest thing I had to one. I didn't have to say a word. She knew this would be a problem for me.

She raised her hand. "Ah, Mr. Weiss, what about those of us who feel that dissection is an unnecessary act of cruelty toward innocent animals that should be banned from all teaching facilities and replaced with computer programs that have been proven to be both a more effective teaching tool and a more frugal use of the school's budgetary allowance?" Kristen was smart. And I don't mean the kind of smart where you make straight A's because you study really hard and do all of your homework. I mean the kind of smart where you make straight A's because you already know what's being taught. I don't know how she got that way. Maybe she put books under her pillow at night and the information magically found its way into her head. She never studied, and I never saw her reading. She just knew things.

"Ms. Emerson," replied Mr. Weiss. "I suggest you keep an open mind about this old-fashioned approach to learning. This is something we all had to do in school. I'm sure your parents had to dissect a mouse to pass biology class, and they weren't permanently scarred from the experience."

A mouse! I thought. *Oh no, I can't.* A frog, maybe, probably not, but at least I could have considered it. But a mouse! I couldn't, not after what I had read in the attic the night before. Kristen grimaced at Mr. Weiss' response to her question.

"Okay, anyone who feels the same as Ms. Emerson about this time-honored approach to teaching and learning, please see me after class."

Billy quickly raised his hand. "Can I get their mouse? Or their mouses?"

"It's mice, Billy, and no you can't," answered Mr. Weiss who was probably running out of patience by this point, but was still hiding it well. I thought it best to keep my aversion to the impending assignment to myself for the moment. I didn't want to be the student who spent the last modicum of patience Mr. Weiss had left. After a deep breath of musty classroom air, Mr. Weiss went on to explain that we would spend the remainder of the week preparing for the dissection. We were going to study a diagram of mouse anatomy on Tuesday, watch a video on mouse dissection Wednesday, and have a question and answer session on Thursday. Friday, we were going to … well, I'd rather not say.

Chapter Four

The Second Set of Pages

Mr. Weiss assigning a dissection project was not the Monday I had expected. Although in hindsight, I've levied my share of complaints about boring school days, this day I would have preferred the academic doldrums of a typical school week to Mr. Weiss' surprise announcement. After reading about Tyne E. and his family the night before, I knew there was no way I could complete the dissection assignment come Friday.

As soon as I got home from school, I climbed the attic ladder hoping desperately to find more pages. I couldn't get the assignment off my mind. I knew I wasn't going to be able to do it, but I hadn't told Mr. Weiss after class like he'd requested. I figured I would talk to Mr. Weiss on Tuesday, but that decision didn't set well with my nerves. I wasn't a procrastinator. If something needed to be done, I had to take care of it right away, or a wave of uneasiness would come over me like a storm front. I'd always been like that. Mom told me it was a sign of maturity. Kristen told me it was a sign of obsessive compulsiveness. I wasn't sure what that meant, but I always liked Granddad's summation of my quirkiness best; he said it was a sign of savviness. That's where I got my nickname. He was the only one who called me Savvy, and I loved the way it sounded.

When I reached the top of the stairs, I pulled the ladder door shut so my mom wouldn't find me. She still didn't know about Granddad's story, and I wasn't ready to tell her yet. Explaining to her that pages were magically appearing in the attic didn't seem like an easy sell. Besides, I needed to conserve my powers of persuasion for when I talked to Mr. Weiss the next day. I opened the trunk, and when I saw a new stack of pages waiting there for me, the storm front that had made all of my nerves feel tingly just moments before began to fade. I picked up the pages and lost myself once again in Granddad's story...

How Tyne E. Met Buddy

Over the years, Tyne E.'s coat saw him through all of life's growing pains. From schoolyard scuffles to his first childhood heartbreak, Tyne E. always remembered what his coat represented. It had become his identity and was what set him apart from other mice. What had once embarrassed Tyne E. had now become his most prized possession and, in part, was responsible for his meeting the most interesting German Shepherd in the world – make that the most interesting *dog* in the world!

"Limitations are no more real than snow snakes and puppy fish!" Buddy would always tell Tyne E.

Well, wait. Maybe I'm getting ahead of myself. Let me slow down and give you a little backdrop. I suppose you need to know how Buddy and Tyne E. came to be such good pals in the first place. After all, it's not often that a German Shepherd and a barn mouse become best friends.

The unlikely pair first met at Eastwood Stables. Eastwood Stables was the largest riding and boarding facility in the entire state. Every inch of the farm was covered in lush green grass as far as the eye could see, with the most magnificent racehorses grazing on it. Row after row of snow-white painted barns, with green trim, set along the tallest hills on the farm. Green wooden letters hung above each set of double barn doors, spelling out the numbers one through nineteen.

Tyne E. lived in Barn Fifteen with his mom, dad, Harry and Tall. Harry had become the proud owner of Cut Tells and Run, the busiest barber shop in all of Eastwood. Tall had become a lawyer and a fine one indeed. Tall was a personal injury lawyer and was known around Eastwood as the best trap chaser a mouse could hire. Although Tall's specialty was personal injury, from time to time he also represented those mice who found themselves in trouble with the Eastwood Mouse Authority. Tall's slogan was, "If you were in a pinch or have been pinched, call me – Tall Tells." It was a pretty catchy slogan, and seeing as he was the best-known lawyer in Eastwood, it must have worked well for him.

Tyne E.'s life had changed a lot from when he was a younger mouse. Tyne E.'s dad's construction company, Building Tells, and Tyne E.'s mom's custom window treatment business, Curtain Tells, had become locally famous. Nearly every mouse in Eastwood Stables knew of the Tells family thanks to a novel idea Mrs. Tells had conceived. When they first moved to the stables, she had insisted that Mr. Tells build her a burrow with windows – the first of its kind in all of Eastwood. When their home was completed, it was the squeak of the stables. Every weekend for two whole months after Mr. and Mrs. Tells finished building their home, the wives of Eastwood dragged their husbands to the Tells' residence, bearing housewarming gifts, in the hope of catching a glimpse of the famous windows. Most of the gifts were homemade baked goodies, which Mr. Tells enjoyed a little too much.

"He has a weakness for sweetness. That's how he ended up with me!" Mrs. Tells jokingly told all of her guests.

When Tyne E. was not helping his mom and dad with the family businesses, he spent most of his free time scurrying about the stables admiring all the racehorses, and that's how he ended up meeting Buddy. The morning Tyne E. first encountered Buddy began like any other. He woke up before everyone else in the burrow and began his trek toward the racetrack. Mornings were the busiest time at Eastwood Stables and the most exciting time of day for Tyne E. It was in the very early hours, before the dew melted from each blade of grass and while a chill still lingered in the morning moonlight, that the splendid racehorses of Eastwood Stables would run their daily workouts. It was Tyne E.'s favorite time of day, but a risky time indeed. All mice in Eastwood knew a trip outside the burrow during morning rush hour was strictly forbidden, but Tyne E. had devised a fail-proof plan for safe travels. He would scurry through the maze of stacked hay bales to the corner of Barn Fifteen and travel through a tunnel to the outside of the barn where he then jumped into the wheel well of the fastest hay cart in all of Eastwood, Milo's.

Every morning Milo, along with nine other farm hands, would come to Barn Fifteen and pick up breakfast for all the racehorses who awaited their fresh hay à la carte – timothy hay for some, alfalfa for others, and coastal for the rest. It didn't take Tyne E. long to figure out his best shot at getting back to the burrow before everyone woke up was to hitch a ride on Milo's cart, and the plan worked superbly – that is, until the morning

Milo's trusted companion detected an unfamiliar scent in his master's hay cart.

Milo didn't always bring Buddy to work with him, but this day was an exception. When they arrived at Eastwood, as Milo got out of his truck, a strong gust of wind caught the door, pressing it back against the hinges. Buddy sat curled in the passenger seat of the truck with his nose tucked tightly against his legs. "Come on, Buddy. It's okay." Milo could see the tips of Buddy's fur swaying from the gusts of wind blowing into the truck. "Come on, boy. Let's go before the rain starts." Milo reached into the truck and grabbed Buddy's collar. Buddy dug his paws into the seat. "Look, I know how scared you are of storms," said Milo, "but we have to go before you make me late. You can stay with me while I make my rounds today. Okay, boy?" Relieved by Milo's promise, Buddy found enough courage to leap from the truck and cautiously head toward the barn.

Bale after bale was tossed onto Milo's cart until it was so full he could barely steer it. "That's good guys," signaled Milo to the barn hands who loaded the carts. "Come on, boy. We've got work to do. Rain or shine, they've gotta eat, right?" Milo asked Buddy, as if to work up the energy to begin his rounds on such a stormy, dreary day.

"Wffff," replied Buddy with a sound that barely qualified as a bark. The two began their rounds, walking from one stall to the next, tossing fresh hay in for the horses. Buddy followed, his head low to the ground but peering up toward the roof of the barn each time he heard thunder in the distance. They didn't even make it halfway through their rounds when a strange scent caught Buddy's attention, and his primal need to investigate relieved him of all his thunderstorm worries. Of course, relief was not the emotion felt by Tyne E. as Buddy's cold, wet nose approached the wheel well of Milo's hay cart. Tyne E. had met only two other dogs in his years as a mousling, and neither of them had been nice. Tyne E., paralyzed with fear at the approaching shiny, black nose, didn't have a clue about what to do. He contemplated jumping off the cart and making a run for it, but he knew Buddy was already too close. As he anxiously weighed his options, he heard a voice.

"Don't worry, I won't say anything," whispered Buddy in a low bowwow mumble. "That is, unless one of the humans is looking. Then I have to bark, because I don't want them thinking I've gone soft in my old age. Just between you and me, I stopped chasing mice years ago. You all are too hard to catch, and I have better things to do with my time. I prefer more gainful endeavors," said Buddy with his nose tilted upward.

Tyne E. froze for a moment in disbelief and thought, *Surely this dog is only kidding*.

"What are you doing here, anyway?" asked Buddy. "Shouldn't you be scurrying around the feed room looking for leftovers, like the other mice do this time of day?" Tyne E. raised his furry brow, squinted his onyx-colored eyes at Buddy and puffed out his chest.

"No! I'm trying to get to the track to watch the horses race, and you're slowing me down. Move your big nose out of my way!" Then Tyne E. reached out his paw and pushed Buddy's nose aside as he jumped down from the wheel well of the cart.

"Well, aren't you a brave one!" said Buddy. "I've never met a mouse with enough gumption to push me out of the way. Typically, in a situation like this, it would cross a dog's mind to eat you in one chomp. But I already told you I wouldn't, and I'm a dog of my word. Plus I ate a minty dental treat earlier, so you probably wouldn't taste quite right."

"It doesn't smell like you just ate a minty dental treat, but if you say so…" said Tyne E. as he scurried away.

"Hey, wait a second," said Buddy. "What's your name, little mouse?"

Tyne E. stopped and replied, "My name is Tyne E. – Tyne E. Tells."

"Well, Tyne E. Tells," said Buddy, "if racing is what you're looking for, then you've met the right dog. Meet me back here tonight at six o'clock sharp. I'll take you to meet the fastest horse you'll ever see."

Tyne E. hesitated for a moment. *He seems like a nice enough dog,* Tyne E. thought. *And I've spent every morning taking chances, sneaking around the stables in broad daylight, so what's another chance? I can't pass up an opportunity like this.*

"Okay," said Tyne E. "Tonight at six, I'll be here."

"Oh, by the way," said Buddy, "lose the coat. I never would have noticed you if it weren't for that coat. It reeks of peanuts."

"Can't do it," answered Tyne E. "I always wear it."

"Suit yourself, friend."

The whole day, Tyne E. could think of nothing but Buddy's promise. The hour hands on the clock passed with slow, steady, rhythmic monotony. Tyne E. could hardly stand the wait. By the time the clock struck five fifty-five, Tyne E. was on his way to find Buddy. Through his well-trodden pathways around the hay bales, Tyne E. scurried out of Barn Fifteen and quickly spotted Buddy.

"Hop under my bandanna, and hold onto my collar, Tyne E.," said Buddy as he walked alongside Milo's cart. "We're almost done for the day. Just stay quiet and don't let yourself be seen. I have to keep up appearances, you know. Being seen smuggling a mouse under my bandanna really would tarnish my watchdog image. And I'm telling you now as fair warning, if you are seen, I plan to bark at you. It's every dog and mouse for himself out here. Can you handle it?"

Tyne E. paused for a brief half second and said, "Yes, let's go." All day Tyne E. had looked forward to Buddy's promise to introduced him to the fastest horse he would ever meet, and a little fear of the unknown was not about to stop him now.

Milo parked the hay cart and motioned for Buddy to follow. "Come on, boy. Let's go home." As they walked along, Tyne E. got to see parts of Eastwood Stables he had never before seen. He peered from underneath Buddy's bandanna with curious amazement. Tyne E. could hardly control his excitement as Buddy leapt into the front seat of Milo's old red truck.

"You're in for a real treat, Tyne E.! Meet Ol' Betsy," woofed Buddy excitedly.

"Who is Ol' Betsy?" Tyne E. asked.

"Why this thing of beauty that's all around you! Just wait till you feel the wind in your fur. Ol' Betsy will take you for a ride faster than any horse around!"

Now, to Tyne E., the 1959 red Dodge pickup would more accurately be described as scrap metal rather than "a thing of beauty," but Buddy was clearly beside himself with excitement. No sooner did Milo put Ol'

Betsy in gear before Tyne E. felt a quick jerk followed by a cool breeze.

"Hang on!" said Buddy as he poked his head outside the truck window and became more and more excited with every small increase in speed. Buddy was clearly in his happy place and Tyne E.? Well, Tyne E. was satisfied to just be along for the ride, at least for now.

Chapter Five

Ten More

I stopped and thumbed through the pages I'd not yet read as if they were inlaid in gold with diamond lettering. Each page was precious to me. My granddad's words had brought me such comfort. I could hear his voice reading to me as my eyes drifted down each page. I wanted there to be hundreds of them, hundreds of pages sitting right in my hands waiting for me to read them all that very night. But instead, there were only ten left. *Ten more*, I thought. *Ten more*. So I savored every word.

"Hop down, boy! It's time to get some dinner," said Milo as he motioned for Buddy to get out of the truck. Tyne E.'s first ride in Ol' Betsy left him looking a little less than dapper. Droplets of Buddy's drool had splashed him every time he peered from under the bandanna, but Tyne E. didn't mind. His excitement for what was to come made him feel as if he were glistening.

"Tyne E., it's supper time!" said Buddy. Dinner was Buddy's second favorite time of the day, behind riding in Ol' Betsy of course. "After we eat, I'll show you around the place." Milo made Buddy's dinner and put his bowl down in front of him. Buddy picked through the bits of food, eating only his favorite flavor first. He stopped with half a bowl left and walked over to the table where Milo sat.

"What are you doing?" asked Tyne E. "You still have half a bowl left."

"This is how you get twice as many treat biscuits. Watch. He'll be putty in my paws. I've been doing this for years, and it works every time," said Buddy. With the persistence and patience of one wholeheartedly devoted to his chosen task, Buddy sat beside Milo and stared at him with unmistakable intent. He did not blink nor flinch one muscle of his body until he had Milo's attention.

"What's the matter, boy? You don't like your food?" Milo got up, walked to the cupboard, and came out with a handful of treat biscuits to add to Buddy's bowl.

"See there," Buddy whispered to Tyne E. as he walked back to his bowl proudly.

Still chewing his mouthful of treat biscuits, Buddy shuffled off toward the door.

"Come on, there's some grain in the barn you can eat. Milo always spills a little when he feeds P. He'll be out right behind us."

"Who's P?" asked Tyne E.

"Oh you'll see," replied Buddy as the two made their way to the barn. Behind them, Tyne E. heard the screen door clack as it closed, followed by a whistle and a thundering gallop. Thump thump, thump thump, thump thump, thump thump. Tyne E. peered into the distance, waiting to see the horse that made such an impressive rumble. He expected to see a towering figure, fit and muscular; but what ran toward him instead was a tall, lanky, and somewhat clumsy-looking horse.

"P is always the first horse in from the pasture at feed time," whispered Buddy. "No other horse can keep up with him."

Beguiled by P's speed, Tyne E.'s eyes widened with amazement.

"Now don't let him see you, Tyne E., because it will scare him," warned Buddy.

"Scare him?" asked Tyne E. "He does know he's a thousand times my size, doesn't he?" All of a sudden Buddy and Tyne E. heard the sound of hooves digging into the dirt. P's feet ripped a path through the pasture grass as he slid to a panicky halt.

"Wha—wha—what's that?" P snorted as he pranced about. "Wha—what's that thing, Buddy? Buddy, there's something on your neck! What is it?"

"Calm down," said Buddy. "This is Tyne E."

Tyne E. jumped down from Buddy's neck. "Tyne E. Tells is the name. Pleased to meet you." Tyne E. had no more said his last name before P bolted sideways, kicking dust and dirt all over both him and Buddy. P ran about twenty feet before he suddenly stopped and turned around to take a second look at the little mouse who had posed such a seemingly dire threat.

You see, Savvy, in addition to being scared of pretty much everything, P was also very indecisive. He second-guessed each and every thought, and this made him one tough horse to ride. Why, even the most experienced and accomplished jockeys who had attempted to ride P swore never to do it again. But there was somebody who still had faith in P, and that somebody was Buddy.

Buddy had recognized P's natural talent for racing the first day the horse arrived on the farm. Buddy knew the only thing P needed was to learn how to run without fear. Once he could do that, he would be able to leave any challenger in the dust. The problem was, Buddy knew he couldn't help P all alone. Buddy needed someone who could ride and talk P through his fears as he raced, someone small and light who wouldn't slow P down with added weight, but also courageous and brave enough to ride P in the first place. Buddy needed fearlessness in a small package. When he met Tyne E., Buddy knew he had found just that.

"So this is the fastest horse I'll ever meet, huh?" said Tyne with a hint of sarcasm. "I'm beginning to think you were only kidding and used that line just to lure me here. Next, I'll probably find out I'm really meant to be one of your treat biscuits, right?"

"I'd hold my judgment if I were you, Tyne E.," said Buddy. "You haven't seen what this horse can do yet. First of all, if you want to be good with horses, if you really want to know a horse, then you have to know his story.

"Let me tell you," said Buddy as he peered off into the distant woods behind the pasture. "This horse has been through a lot, and if it weren't for my keen nose and my gift of persuasion, he might still be lost in those woods right there."

Somewhat concerned, but mostly just curious, Tyne E. asked eagerly, "Well, what happened?"

"Now you want to know more, huh? Take a seat in that pile of hay, and I'll tell you all you need to know about that night."

After gathering bits of spilt grain to munch on, Tyne E. settled into a pile of golden hay in the corner of P's stall, and Buddy began to tell Tyne E. all about his first encounter with P.

"One evening as Milo and I headed home from Eastwood, we spotted a black and white paint horse trotting awkwardly down the road. Milo could tell right away the horse was hurt, because he was favoring his right front hoof. So Milo pulled over and told me to stay in the truck as he grabbed a rope from behind the seat. He tied a few knots as fast as his fingers would let him. I could tell he was nervous because he dropped the rope three times before he finished the knots, but when he was done, the rope had somehow become a halter. I'd never seen him do that before. I'd seen him turn a rope into a leash plenty of times, but never a halter. When he finished, he began to walk toward the horse, who had stopped just ahead of us. I think the horse was as curious about us as we were about him. I tried to follow, but Milo put his hand up and told me to stay. I didn't have much of a choice at that point. His tone was far more serious than normal, and I didn't want to be the reason we couldn't catch and help the horse. He obviously needed someone's help, and I mean he needed it badly. When Milo got close, I saw him look down toward the horse's hoof, and that's when I realized his hoof was bleeding. The poor guy was a real mess. His mane was knotted, and he was drenched with perspiration. Milo eased toward him and whispered 'Easy boy,' under his breath. Then, much to my surprise, the horse lowered his head all the way to the ground and rested his muzzle against the sand. Even from the truck I could see water dripping from his nostrils and sweat rolling down his neck.

"'Easy now,' whispered Milo. 'I'm not going to hurt you. I need to put this halter on you so I can look at that hoof.' I watched eagerly as Milo touched the horse for the first time. He ran his hand along the muscles of the horse's neck, and when the horse lifted his head just a little, Milo slid the bottom end of the halter over the horse's muzzle and draped the remaining rope over the horse's ears. As Milo tied the knot to secure the halter, I heard him give a deep sigh of relief. He tightened the knot and began leading the horse toward Ol' Betsy and me. I thought everything was going to be fine at that moment, but let me tell you, Tyne E., boy was I wrong!

"I heard it before Milo, of course, but it was coming toward us so quickly that it wasn't long before he heard it, too. It was an eighteen-wheeler, a gargantuan truck. As the truck drew closer, I watched the horse tilt his ears forward and quickly raise his head. Wide-eyed, the horse stared at the truck and stood perfectly still, not moving one muscle in his body. I readied myself like an Olympic sprinter at the starting line waiting for the BANG. I knew what was about to happen, and I suppose Milo did too, because I saw him tighten his grip on the lead rope. Then, a wall of wind hit us as if the truck had extendable hands to smack roadside onlookers. The huge truck sped past us so quickly that the ground shook. Milo tried to steady the horse, but there was no use. 'Whoa, whoa, whoa!' Milo yelled, but before he even finished the third whoa, the horse was already forty feet away, entering the wood line.

"That was my cue. The BANG had sounded, even if it was only in my head. I leapt from the truck window without wasting a second. Milo yelled, 'No, Buddy! Stay!' but I couldn't resist the urge to chase the horse. Honestly, I felt a little guilty running away from Milo after he'd told me to stay. It really wasn't like me to do something like that, but I knew if I didn't go after the horse, he might get lost in the woods, and well, who knows what would have become of him."

Buddy's gaze fixated on the remaining bits of grain Tyne E. had not yet eaten. He lifted his right hind foot and began to scratch behind his ear. Tyne E. waited for Buddy to stop scratching and continue his story, but Tyne E.'s impatience got the better of him.

"Well?" urged Tyne E.

"Well what?" replied Buddy, still scratching.

"What happened then? Did you catch him?"

"Oh! Of course I did. I may not be able to run as fast as a horse, but I won't be outwitted by one. I just put my nose to the ground and went to work." Buddy finally stopped scratching. He stood up and shook the loose bits of hay off his fur.

"Ah, hay! I don't know how you lie in this stuff. It makes me so itchy."

"So what happened when you caught up with the horse?" Tyne E. asked eagerly.

"Well, luckily I didn't have to run very far before I found him. I was probably about two hundred yards into the woods when my nose picked up his scent. I followed it until I heard leaves rustling back and forth. When I lifted my head, I saw a big horse rump shivering and shaking behind a small thicket of brush. I really wasn't sure what to say, so I just coughed under my breath hoping he would lift his head from behind the bushes. But, when subtlety failed, I decided a proper introduction might be a better way to go. So I said my name and waited, and waited, and waited some more.

"I was beginning to think he wasn't ever going to answer when I finally heard,
'There isn't anyone here, especially not a horse. No, no horses here. I am quite sure of it.'

"Perplexed by the horse's response, I replied, 'But I can see you, you know. I can see all but your head. That's a pretty small shrub, and you're a pretty tall horse. Perhaps you can lift your head, and we'll have proper introductions.' Then I asked him his name.

"'I can't recall,' said the horse. 'Oh, P! I think. It is P then something, or is it something then P? I'm really not sure. I just know there is a P in it somewhere. Oh no, I've gone and done it again. I've had the wits scared out of me. The last time this happened, I couldn't remember my name for months!'

"I told him it was fine that he'd forgotten his name, and we both agreed that P would work just as well until he could remember the rest. I knew we needed to get his hoof looked at soon, so I convinced him to follow me home, and I howled ahead to let Doc and Bird know we were on our way."

"Wait a second," interrupted Tyne E. "Doc and Bird?"

"Oh that's right! You haven't met Doc or Bird yet. Well you will, and when you do, you'll never forget them. They're quite the duo. Doc is our resident veterinarian, and Bird assists him, or tolerates him, depending on the day. I'd introduce you now, but they're out on a barn call. The neighbor three doors down has a mare in her pasture that's about to birth a foal at any moment." Buddy gazed toward the ground. His head swiveled back and forth like a pendulum on a grandfather clock. He conjured a toothy canine grin. "Goodness, I sure hope your first meeting with Doc is as entertaining as P's."

"What do you mean," asked Tyne E.? "It went well, right?"

"Absolutely! That's one way of putting it."

"So?" Tyne E. leaned in awaiting Buddy's explanation.

"When we finally reached the farm, I rushed P into the first empty stall I could find so that Doc could examine him. I hadn't even got P completely in the stall before I heard, 'Oh my, this is quite the case, quite the case indeed! My first zebra! Ah yesssss. Quick, get the soda pop and apply it to the abrasions. The bubbles will kill the germs.'

"'Actually, I'm a horse – a paint horse. But where is that voice coming from?' asked P, as he looked all around the stall.

"'I'm here, Zebra. Look up, on the top of the door,' the voice said loudly. On the top of the stall door, near the metal hinge, sat Doc, the fattest, hairiest caterpillar in all of veterinary medicine. 'Trust me, you are a zebra,' he insisted. 'Black, white, four hooves: yes sir, you are a zebra indeed! My spectators please, Bird,' requested Doc.

I introduced Doc and Bird to P hoping to ease P's nerves a bit, but honestly, I think my nerves were more frayed than P's by that point. You know, I can't recall Bird's real name. I've only ever heard Doc refer to him as Bird, and Bird doesn't seem to mind the nickname. Besides, Doc tends to have his own names for many things. He speaks a language all his own, and Bird is the only one who can understand Doc's particular sort of genius."

"Buddy," said Tyne E.

"I know, I know, I digress. After proper introductions, Doc spouted, 'Bird, I do not have all day. Place the spectators upon my nose so that I may examine this here zebra.' And with that, Bird placed Doc's glasses on his nose and the examination began. 'Thank you, Bird. First things first, Zebra, I will need to listen to your ticker. Take ten paces forward.' A bit confused, but willing to oblige, P took ten steps forward. Click clack, click clack, click clack, click clack, click clack.

"'Your pace is magnificent, Zebra. There will be no pacemaker required. Bird, I will not need my telescope for this examination. The patient's ticker is clearly ticking. Now for your ear inspection, Zebra – Bird, hoist me, so that I may now examine the zebra's ears.' Bird then picked up Doc in his beak and placed him on the top of P's right ear. 'Yes! I hear it.' Doc declared.

"'You hear what?' asked P.

"'The waves. The ocean can be heard in this zebra's ears clearly. Mark him down for 20/20 hearing, Bird. Now, for your eye examination, Zebra: how many doctors do you see?' asked Doc.

"'Um, one?' replied P as if to ask more than to answer.

"'Bird, get him a lolli! Zebra, you have passed your examination with flying colors! When the soda pop stops bubbling, Bird will place a bandage on your scratches. Bird, the lolli!' yelled Doc impatiently.

"'Oh that won't be necessary, really,' P said as Bird flew overhead delivering the lolli. Bird handed P a straight blade of hay with an adjoining blade tied to the top in a perfect bow.

"'Nonsense, zebra, all of my patients get a lolli after an examination,' boasted Doc as Bird placed him atop the stall door.

"P hesitantly took the lolli, thanks to my inconspicuous motioning for him to do so, and thus began his first night of many here in this old barn." Buddy gazed across the barn, recollecting memories of untold stories, reliving them in a memory bank to which only he held the key. His eyes perused the planks of cobweb-covered, splintered, cypress wood that made up the barn walls.

"Buddy?" whispered Tyne E. breaking the silence carefully and inquisitively. "How did he get on the road that day in the first place? You never did say."

Buddy abruptly stopped studying the walls of the barn and focused all of his attention on Tyne E.

"That's because he's never told me," replied Buddy. "I figure the important part is that he's here now. When P is ready to tell the rest of his story, he will."

"Why don't you ask him?" said Tyne E. "Don't you want to know? It's not every day you see a horse walking down the road alone – a dog, maybe, but not a horse."

"Of course I want to know. But he's not ready to tell yet, and I don't want to rush him," explained Buddy. "Look, Tyne E., I'm trying to be considerate. P has sensitive feelings, the kind you have to tiptoe around and use amounts of consideration you've probably never imagined. I don't want to ask him before he's ready. That would be rude."

"Feelings schmeelings." Tyne E. waved his paw in disagreement. "How do you know he's not ready to talk about it? I'll ask him now."

"Tyne E., no!" Buddy shook his head flapping his one crooked ear. "Where are your manners?"

As if Buddy had not said a thing, Tyne E. yelled, "Hey P, what's your story? Where are you from?"

"Oh thank you, thank you, thank you! I've been here all this time, and no one has ever asked me that!" P smacked his lips eagerly and swallowed a mouthful of thick, green pasture grass. "I was beginning to think no one cared."

Tyne E. looked at Buddy as if to say *I told you so*, and Buddy looked at Tyne E. with an expression words can't fully express.

"P, I thought you had amnesia," said Buddy.

"Well, I used to, but that went away last week," said P. "I'm fine now."

"Why didn't you tell me?" asked Buddy.

"You never asked me," replied P.

Buddy, deciding to give up on logical conversational reasoning, just smiled and said, "Okay, P. We're all ears. Where are you from?"

"Mr. Cheatham's," P mumbled indistinctly between bites of pasture grass.

"Mr. Cheatham's! You belong to old mean Cheatham!" said Tyne E. in disbelief. "And you actually made it out of there?"

"Mmmmhmm," affirmed P as he munched along.

"Wait a second, who is old mean Cheatham?" asked Buddy.

"Mr. Cheatham is the meanest man in horseracing," replied Tyne E. "His horses win all the time, but it's always at a price."

"Yeah, a price I'm not will to pay anymore," said P, tossing his head in a firm, decisive nod.

"Why? What did he do to you?" asked Buddy.

"They did all sorts of things to make us horses run faster. They used whips on my rear end and electric buzzers on my neck. Why, they even poked me with a nail one time to make me bolt toward the finish line," said P, with a tear in his eye and grass stuck to his lips.

P paused for a moment and gazed into the distance. "Hey, these questions are kind of personal, don't you think? I mean, I can't believe you're asking. Do I even know you two fellas?"

"Oh no," said Buddy, shaking his head. "His amnesia is back."

"Buddy," said Tyne E. "This horse is a fruitcake. But I like him! Do you think I could ride him?"

Chapter Six

P to Pepper

Tyne E.'s question to Buddy played over and over in my mind as I drifted to sleep that night. If Tyne E. was brave enough to ride P, then I could certainly talk to Mr. Weiss the next day and explain to him that mouse dissection simply wasn't for me. I decided it would be that easy.

During the ride to school the next morning, Mom stayed on the phone the entire time, which was actually a huge relief. I still wasn't ready to tell her about the story. I spent most of the ride staring out of my window at the passing trees. Each tall, skinny pine flashed by my sight like cards in a deck whose corners had been bent back and then released by the skilled, perfectly-timed thumb of a Vegas blackjack dealer. My mind felt as if it were being poked by an irritating little sibling, and I knew the badgering wouldn't stop until I talked to Mr. Weiss and got excused from doing his ridiculous assignment. I mean, *it's archaic, it's barbaric, it's inhumane! Why would anyone ever want to dissect a poor little…*

TAP, TAP, TAP. The nail on my Mom's left index finger was unusually strong and was very effective at interrupting my thoughts. The force she could use on that thin nail to direct my attention to something on the other side of the car window was always surprising to me. I actually tried it myself one day. I wanted to see if I could make that same loud tap, and you know what? It hurt. It really hurt. Mom curled her fingers in the shape of a circle and motioned at me as if she were eating. While still talking on the phone, she gesticulated the entire act of stopping at the old bait and tackle for donut holes and finished up her silent conversation with a thumbs up and a thumbs down.

"No, I'm fine," I whispered. She pushed out her bottom lip and straightened her brow. She knew it wasn't like me to turn down breakfast. What twelve-year-old would pass up donut holes? I loved them. I could have eaten them every day if Mom would have allowed it, just not today. "I'm fine, Mom. Just not very hungry, that's all." She put her hand on my shoulder and squeezed my arm while the dimple in her right cheek deepened with the soft smile she sent my way, another gesture, this time meaning *I love you*. In that short moment, I felt as I had when I was beside the trunk reading Granddad's story. It was as if I'd seen him in her briefly. Her smile was kind like his. The glow of light in her eye was warm like his. It was like he was there with me in that moment, that brief moment. But however brief, the moment was exactly what I needed as our car approached the towering front doors of Ward Middle.

When I got to school, the bell that haunted all Ward Middle students had just unleashed its electronic chiming fury on every hearing ear.

"Ugh, I can't take it. That stupid bell," declared Kristen as I slipped into my seat while Ms. Borellis once again called roll backwards.

"Here!" I chimed. Ms. Borellis glanced my way and smiled.

"So, did you do any more reading last night?" asked Kristen. I had told her about the trunk during lunch the previous day. She knew all about the note, about the messenger, and about Tyne E. While Ms. Borellis took the lunch count, I filled Kristen in on what I had read the night before, and we conspired on how best to approach Mr. Weiss about my being excused from the dissection assignment. We didn't get too far into our scheme before we heard a ringing in the halls. This was not the same toenail-curling, goose-bump-evoking, chill-causing, shrill alarm that we were used to hearing this time of day. No, instead, this was almost pleasant. Almost.

"Students, leave your book bags and belongings and line up as we practiced," ordered Ms. Borellis who rarely *ordered* anything. She wasn't that type of teacher. She was the requesting type; the type that you always knew you could push further than most. But she was so kind that you seldom, if ever, actually did. Everyone lined up without hesitation – even the cheerleaders who I would have expected to frantically grab their purses. At least that was what had happened during the last drill. The bell rang and everyone immediately took their places in line, with the exception of the four-strong squad who insisted Ms. Borellis wait for them to gather their personal essentials, which consisted of credit cards, cell phones, and varying shades of lip gloss. That time Ms. Borellis had seemed perfectly content to oblige the clique of fashion-forward beauty-conscious girls, but this time was noticeably different. It was as if the entire class had sensed a hint of urgency in her voice and knew her uncharacteristic tone meant this was no drill.

By the time Ms. Borellis reached for the knob of the classroom door, I could see smoke seeping under the crack at the bottom. She said, "Follow me. Stay in line, single file. Everyone hold the hand of the person behind you and don't let go." The closest exit was the main entrance to the school. I knew that was where we were headed. When Ms. Borellis opened the door, the smoke loomed in the hall like a thick, sticky paste. The air that had only moments ago been filled with the papery aroma of books, the metallic odor of rusty lockers, and the funk of Billy Marshall's first period gym shoes had been sucked up by the all-consuming presence of grey billows. Although I didn't want to show it, I was scared. No one said a word. If anyone in the class had missed the serious tone of Ms. Borellis' voice, they were quickly made aware of the gravity of the situation soon after she opened the door. I couldn't see the person in front of me. All I knew was that he or she had my left hand and Kristen had my right.

Ms. Borellis' classroom was only two rooms down from the main school entrance, but on the opposite side of the hall. Those tall, double glass doors were all I could think about as we, in perfect single file, cut through the smoky haze. When we reached the doors, the dense grey smoke lessened, and the source of the morning's chaos became apparent. Ms. Borellis' classroom was positioned beside the cafeteria. It seemed our class had suffered the brunt of an accidental grease fire that fortunately never got too out of control, a bacon-burning catastrophe averted. At least that's what the gossip was among the students as we all congregated in our predetermined "safety" zones.

In a smoke-coated, scratchy voice of disdain, Kristen lamented, "You know, I can't even believe they're still serving us bacon. It's the twenty-first century, and this school is crispy-frying an animal that's smarter than a dog! Did you know some studies have shown pigs are even smarter than dolphins and three-year-olds? Ugh, I can't even think about it!"

The bacon was not on the radar of my concerns but I listened. After all, Kristen's activism was going to help me with my mouse dilemma, so the least I could do was sympathize with her aversion to pork consumption.

"Have a seat in the grass, kids," instructed Ms. Borellis. Each teacher was meticulously counting heads as the school nurse moved from group to group offering her help to anyone who felt they needed it. No one looked as if they needed anything, except for one sandy-haired boy who must have had asthma. He was wheezing pretty badly, but once he got his inhaler, he seemed fine.

"Well, I guess we should get comfortable. This could take a while," murmured Kristen as she checked the grass for ants before planting herself in the cleanest spot she could find. I sat down next to her, with no real mind for what was underneath me. I was distracted by the conversation Ms. Borellis was having with one of the other teachers about whether school would be cancelled for the remainder of the day. From what I could gather, the fire hadn't been all that bad, but the school needed a good airing out before we would be allowed back inside. The fire trucks howled in the distance. I could see them just beginning to turn onto the road that ran alongside the football field.

"Hey," Kristen bumped my arm with her elbow. "Have you ever thought...oh, never mind."

"Thought what?"

"Well, just that, that maybe the pages you keep finding in the trunk are, well..."

"Yes?"

"Are, you know, being put there by your mom." Kristen shrugged diffidently.

What? I was appalled. *How could she? How could she doubt me? She was my best friend.* But before I even had a chance to respond, Kristen quickly relented. She must have seen the expression of disapproval that covered my entire face like a mask. I could, when times called for it, control my words, but my expressions were another matter altogether. My feelings and my face were intertwined. One could not hide from the other no matter how hard my brain tried to make them.

"I'm sorry," she said. "If you say the pages are coming from your grandfather, then I believe you. I shouldn't have even suggested otherwise."

"It's all right," I replied, choking down a lump of resentment that had quickly formed in my throat. "I know it's hard to believe. I don't understand it myself. I just know it's happening."

"Okay, so let's try to figure it out. Why would your grandfather be sending you pages to read each night? Maybe it's a message."

"Or maybe it's just a story," I suggested, knowing in my heart that was not the case. Of course it wasn't *just a story*. Stories came from bookstores and library shelves. They didn't spontaneously appear in magical trunks. My heart told me there was a story beyond the story, but my head told me to *play it cool or you'll look crazy*.

"You used to spend a lot of time with your granddad before he got sick, right?"

"Yeah."

"You were there every summer."

"Yeah."

"Well, did you ever see him writing?"

"No, I never did. That's what makes this whole thing even harder to understand. It's like everything changed all at once. Things were normal, and then I wasn't allowed to go there anymore."

"To your granddad's farm?"

"Yeah, after the whole Pepper incident, things were never the same."

"Pepper incident?"

"Yes, Pepper. She was a horse at Granddad's farm. She was a baby, a strawberry roan."

"What's a strawberry roan?"

"It's like a redhead in the horse world. She was beautiful. Her coat was white

with shades of orange that covered her like rainbow sprinkles. Her mane was rust-colored near her neck and faded to blonde at the tips. She wasn't like any of the other foals on Granddad's farm. Granddad had tried to win her over lots of times, but none of them went as he'd hoped. I was the only person Pepper would let near her."

"So what happened?" Kristen asked. "You've never said anything about this until today."

Kristen was right. Before that day, I hadn't told her, or anyone else for that matter. No one knew about what had happened except for my granddad and me. I didn't talk about it, because I knew it was unpleasant for my granddad. He blamed himself even though I knew he shouldn't.

"Well…" I paused. I didn't want to tell the story, but Kristen *was* my best friend. If I couldn't talk to her, then who could I talk to? So I took a deep breath, gathered the courage I needed to face the unpleasant memory, and began to tell her what had happened on that cold December night. "You remember two years ago when I missed a week of school right after Christmas break?"

"Yeah, I remember that. You said you had a bad cold. I remember having to make copies of my history notes for you to use, so you wouldn't get behind in class."

"Right. Well, I never told you the whole story, the reason I got sick in the first place. It wasn't really anybody's fault; it's just one of those things that happens. I guess if it had been anyone's fault, it would have been mine, but Granddad didn't see it that way. He was always so strict about me being in the pastures when he wasn't around, and I sort of understood why. The horses were big, fast, unpredictable at times, but I knew they would never hurt me. So every night, after I was sure Granddad had gone to sleep, I would sneak out to visit them. Pepper was just a baby, and I was still trying to earn her trust. She had come up to me a few times and touched my hand with her muzzle, but that was it. The nighttime was when I felt I had the best chance of proving to her that I was her friend. It was quiet and peaceful, and there weren't all the distractions of the day to pull her away from me.

"Before going out that night, I had filled my pockets with peppermints for Pepper and a few Ritz crackers for myself. I figured if she saw me eating, she might want to try some, too. Like always, I was really quiet when I left the house, turning the knob before I closed the door behind me so Granddad wouldn't hear the loud click it made. I tiptoed down the porch steps and headed toward the pasture.

"I remember thinking that something was different. That night was unusually cold, and the air was wet with a chill that soaked right through my coat. I made it halfway to the pasture gate before realizing I couldn't hear Pepper. Even when there wasn't enough moonlight to spot her with my eyes, I could always hear her chomping grass, blowing air through her lips, or even nickering sometimes. The logical side of me thought maybe she had found a warm spot to lie down, but the intuitive side of me triggered a chill even worse than the one brought on by the wet air. As I got closer to the gate, the moonlight glistened off the silver-toned safety latch, and I realized why I couldn't hear her. The gate was open. I instantly panicked. My first thought was to wake Granddad and tell him Pepper had got loose but I was scared. I didn't want to get in trouble. Plus, I'd convinced myself it was entirely possible for me to find her on my own. I knew that farmland and the woods around it as well as Granddad did, and Pepper was much more likely to come to me than to anyone else. So I began to walk.

"At first it wasn't so bad out there in the woods by myself. I felt like I was doing something really important. I was on a rescue mission, an adventure. But it didn't take long before one step turned into one hundred, and I began to lose my way. I thought I knew the woods, but darkness has a way of playing tricks on your memory. The big oak with the lazy limb that resembled a limp arm seemed to have disappeared. I had always used it as a marker to find my way out of the woods. I tried to stay on the narrow deer paths, but as the woods thickened, even those became hard to follow. Before I knew it, I found myself tangled in a dense thicket of brush. Thorns surrounded me. Their sharp points faced me like slivers of metal being drawn toward a magnet. My coat kept my arms from being too scratched, but my hair got tangled in the long thorns. It seemed like the more I moved, the tighter the thicket held me, and I became trapped.

"I've never been more scared in my life. No one knew I was there. Granddad wouldn't realize Pepper and I were both missing until morning, and I didn't know how I was going to make it through the night. I was freezing. I have never been that cold before, and I never want to be that cold again. I can remember trying not to shiver because the movement caused the thorns to pierce deeper through my clothes and into my skin. It was awful."

I felt my face flush as I relived the memory for Kristen. My throat began to feel full, and I stared at the blurry ground through watery, tear-filled eyes. I didn't want Kristen, or anyone else for that matter, to see me cry, so I coolly brushed the sleeve of my sweatshirt across my face, more akin to the way someone would wipe sweat from their brow than to the way one would dry watery eyes.

"How did you get loose?" Kristen asked softly. "I mean, if you don't mind telling me." I could see the concern in her eyes, her wrinkled brow, in the way she drew nearer to me as if my words had hooked her ear and pulled her close.

"I honestly don't know. That's the amazing part of the story. Sometime in the night, I fell asleep. The next morning, I woke up to the sound of barking and an unusual sort of warmth. The air was prickly cold, the ground was covered in frosty crystals of ice, but I felt as warm as I would have if I'd slept in my own bed. That's when she nickered."

"Pepper?"

"Yes. She was curled up next to me on the ground. She must have pulled me out of the thicket sometime in the middle of the night. She was the only thing that kept me from freezing that night. I remember feeling her stomach vibrate with every nicker."

"She was calling to your granddad, wasn't she?"

"Yeah. It's pretty amazing when you think about it. I can remember my eyelids being heavy and sticky, but when I finally managed to open them, I could see Granddad's fuzzy figure running toward us with his dog leading the way. Pepper never moved. She lay perfectly still until Granddad reached down and pulled me from the nest of leaves she and I had slept in that night.

"That was the last time I ever stayed at my granddad's farm. The next week I came down with a bad cold and missed five whole days of school. The first weekend after I got better, I asked Mom if I could stay at Granddad's, and she said no. She said Granddad was scared he wouldn't be able to keep me safe because he was beginning to forget things."

"Maybe that's when he started writing," said Kristen. "You said you never saw him writing. Maybe he wrote you the story because you couldn't be there with him. Maybe the story was his way of being with you when he couldn't."

Suddenly it became apparent. Why hadn't I realized this before? Kristen was right. Granddad's story was his way of being with me not only then, but now, too. He had found a way to make the impossible possible. Just like Tyne E. was determined to become a jockey against all odds, Granddad was determined to be with me even after he got sick. It made perfect sense now, and it made me want to race home to look for more pages.

Chapter Seven

The Third Set of Pages

Luckily for me, and for every student at Ward Middle, the rest of Tuesday's classes were called off to allow time for the school to air out after the kitchen fire. The entire student body jubilantly went home early. I couldn't have been happier to get home to my attic, with one exception. I still hadn't talked to Mr. Weiss about his barbaric dissection assignment. I knew there was nothing I could do about it until the next day, and I had worried myself enough the night before to count for two nights. So I decided tonight wasn't going to be about worry. Tonight was going to be about the third set of pages Granddad's messenger had left for me. With that thought,

I climbed into the attic, found what I knew would be waiting for me, and began to read…

The Mouse Jockey

Over the following weeks, Tyne E. spent nearly all his time with Buddy and P. Every evening, just before time for Milo to leave Eastwood, Tyne E. scurried out to Ol' Betsy and sneaked into the cab where he'd hitch a ride to Milo's farm. Tyne E. had finally found his opportunity to do what he'd always dreamed – to ride a horse. Until his friendship with P, Tyne E. had only been able to watch the horses from within the shadows, hidden away from the humans at Eastwood who would have welcomed him with the swat of a broom.

Every day Tyne E. begged and pleaded with P. "Come on, P. I know I can do it. I'll just sit between your ears and hold onto your mane. Just let me try."

It took persistence, but Tyne E. eventually convinced P that he could ride.

After the first ride, Tyne E. was hooked! He and P went on rides every evening after feeding time. Tyne E. was a natural rider. He used P's forelock (the hair that lay between his eyes) as makeshift reins. When Tyne E. wanted P to turn right, he pulled the hair on the right side of P's forelock. When Tyne E. wanted P to turn left, he pulled the hair on the left side of P's forelock. For everything else Tyne E. wanted P to do, he simply asked. Because Tyne E. sat between P's ears, P could hear everything Tyne E. said, otherwise, his small voice would have been drowned out by the pounding of P's hooves. Their system worked beautifully, with the exception of one small glitch: P's chronic and ill-timed amnesia.

P's amnesia came and went without warning or good reason, and when it kicked in while Tyne E. was between P's ears, Tyne E. got the ride of his life. The first time it happened, Tyne E. managed to hold on as P kicked, bucked, and bolted. P must have run a full mile before finally stopping and realizing that it was his friend

Tyne E. clutching onto his mane for dear life and not a scary monster. It was a real problem for Tyne E. until one day he came up with a clever solution. Tyne E. decided to tell P the voice he heard was his own thoughts – his inner racehorse.

After that, Tyne E. could ride P better than the most talented and gifted jockeys in all of horse racing. The two had a connection that would have been rivaled by even the very best in the sport. They were a dynamic duo, the fastest horse ridden by the smartest – and lightest, might I add – jockey in all of history!

With Tyne E. riding P every day, P grew even stronger and faster than he was when he raced for Mr. Cheatham. He was an exceptional racehorse already, but the daily workouts, minus the cruel methods old mean Mr. Cheatham used, really improved P's strength, speed, and confidence. Anyone who knew anything about racing would have dropped their jaw in awe to see P run with Tyne E. at the reins. And that is exactly what happened the first morning Milo caught sight of the unlikely pair.

Tyne E., the stowaway, had hitched a ride in Ol' Betsy the night before to spend the weekend with Buddy and P. Not usually a morning mouse, Tyne E. woke up this particular Saturday morning full of energy and ready to ride.

Milo, as he did every morning, stumbled to the kitchen toward his coffeepot, which sat right beneath a window overlooking the pasture.

As Milo placed the filter in the coffeepot, something caught his eye. He didn't pay much attention at first until he heard the pounding of hooves outside the window. When Milo looked up and focused his eyes, what he saw was anything but ordinary. There was P, galloping along with a mouse between his ears holding tightly to his mane with one paw and pointing in the direction he wanted P to go with the other. Milo dropped his coffee cup and ran to the door to get a better look. By the time Milo put on his coat and ran outside, P and Tyne E. were in the middle of the pasture. Tyne E. had P doing figure eights in the grass as Milo watched in amazement. He didn't believe what he was seeing – a mouse jockey.

Scared he would startle the mouse, Milo decided to sneak back inside to watch the unlikely pair.

"To the left," Tyne E. shouted to P. "Now the right." P galloped along making perfect figure eights in the pasture grass. "Four paces then slide to a stop."

Milo knew if he didn't get proof of what he was seeing, no one would ever believe him. Frantically, he rushed to the bedroom where, in his nightstand, he kept an old Polaroid camera his mom had given him years ago. Shuffling his socked feet swiftly across the wooden floors, he nearly slipped on his way back to the kitchen. As he slid across the floor, he hurriedly unzipped the camera case. Hoping the batteries were still good, he lifted the camera and tried to bring P and the mouse jockey into focus, but P and Tyne E. were too far away to take a clear picture. Milo snapped the shot, in spite of the blurred view, and ran outside to get a better look. Trying his absolute best to go unnoticed, Milo tiptoed to the corner of the barn where he stood behind a large round bale of hay and took snapshots of P being ridden by the world's smallest jockey.

Click! Click!

"Do you hear that sound?" Doc asked Bird as he munched on a leaf Bird had brought him for breakfast. "Go check it out, Bird."

When Bird flew around the corner, he saw Milo kneeling behind a bale of hay, camera in hand, ready to take another round of pictures. Behind Milo's left foot was a stack of Polaroid pictures that had yet to develop. Bird knew immediately that the situation was dire. He knew he had to snatch up those pictures before Milo had a chance to show them to anyone. It was the only way to keep P safe without old Mr. Cheatham finding him.

As Milo took the next picture, Bird swooped down and flapped his wings right over Milo's head, causing a huge ruckus. Bird dove down at warp speed and tried to grab the stack of pictures with his beak, but there were too many. The pictures scattered on the ground under Milo's feet as he waved his arms in the air, shooing away his unwanted visitor. Bird knew there was no way he would be able to get to the pictures with Milo flailing his arms, so he resorted to his only option. He needed a distraction, and the only thing he knew would work for certain was the one thing he hated having to do…

SPLAT.

Milo ran his fingers through his hair, knowing that what he was about to find would not be pretty. "Doggone it!" he shouted as he ran over to the water hose to rinse Bird's gift from his hair. Ready to seize his opportunity, Bird landed on the ground next to the stack of scattered pictures and managed to pick up every one of them in his beak. Just as Bird flapped his wings to take off with the stack of photos, he felt a gust of wind and something brush against his tail feathers.

"Oh no you don't," said Milo as he tried to get his pictures from Bird. Milo swatted at Bird and stumbled around as water from his wet hair dripped into his eyes. Milo tried with all his might to get his pictures back from Bird, but it was no use. Bird had flown too high for Milo to reach. Milo looked up. Just as he thought all was lost, one stray picture fell from the sky and hit his nose.

In the meantime, Bird headed back to the barn to tell Doc all about the encounter he'd just had and to show him the photographs.

"What's that you have there, Bird?" Doc asked as Bird landed atop the stall door where Doc sat munching on his breakfast. "Oh my, oh my indeed!" Doc exclaimed. Bird nodded his head in agreement.

"They've come," said Doc. "I knew they would. I knew word would get out that I have saved a zebra. You know, Bird, treating a zebra patient is far more complicated than treating the common horse patient. It takes the utmost skill and expertise. No wonder the paparazzi has arrived. Quick, how do I look? Is my fuzz in place?"

Just then P came rushing into the stall with Tyne E. riding between his ears.

"Doc, did you see it?" asked Tyne E. with excitement. "Bird swooped and dove and flapped his wings! He was amazing."

"That's nice that you flew and all, Bird, but the paparazzi are here to see me, not you," said Doc. He turned to Tyne E. and whispered, "I will have to break this to him gently."

"You see, Bird, my talents are many…" Doc began to say. Tyne E. interrupted him while shaking his head.

"Milo took these pictures," said Tyne E.

"Milo!" replied Doc. "Milo has joined the paparazzi?"

"No," said Tyne E. "He must have seen us in the pasture this morning. All I know is that those pictures can never get out. If anyone who knows Cheatham sees those pictures, then P is leaving here for sure. We're lucky Bird snatched them up when he did."

Meanwhile, unbeknownst to the entire crew, Milo had managed to dust off the one stray picture that Bird had dropped. He stuffed it into his pocket.

"I can't believe this," muttered Milo as he walked toward the house. "What a morning. First, I see a mouse riding my horse, then a crazy bird attacks me. The guys at work are going to love this story."

"Buddy! Come on, boy. The weather man says it's supposed to storm this afternoon, so you're coming with me today," Milo yelled. He stood by the front door waiting for Buddy who was sleeping the morning away curled up on the couch.

Buddy spent the entire day by Milo's side, completely unaware of the morning's events. When Milo took his afternoon break, Buddy overheard Milo telling one of his friends about a mouse and a horse. Buddy knew right away that Milo had spotted Tyne E. riding P.

"No seriously, the mouse was actually riding my horse. Here, I have a picture," said Milo to his friends as he reached into his pocket.

When Buddy overheard Milo, he immediately went into guard dog mode. Buddy knew P's fate depended upon keeping his presence at Milo's farm a secret, and the picture Milo was about to pull from his pocket would have ruined everything. Buddy felt his heart skip a beat as Milo fumbled through his pants pockets.

"Well, I thought it was here. I just had it this morning. I must have left it in the pocket of my jacket in the truck," said Milo as his friends ribbed him about his vivid imagination. Milo knew no one was ever going to believe him without proof, but his afternoon break was almost over, and he didn't have time to run to his truck to get the picture.

"It's in my truck, so I'll have to get it when we clock out," said Milo to his friends. "Meet me back here after work. I'll have the picture."

Buddy knew this was his chance. He had three hours to get to that picture before Milo did, and he was determined to do it. He just didn't know exactly how. What he did know was the doors on Ol' Betsy were always locked; and, without thumbs, there was no way he could open the doors on his own. He needed help. He needed Tyne E.

Chapter Eight

Can't Stop Now

I had just picked up the next page to find out how Buddy was going to get the picture from Milo's truck when I heard, "Savannah. Savannah, where are you?" I could hear Mom's footsteps as she headed down the hall toward my room.

"Savannah!" I was hesitant to answer right away, because I didn't want her to know I was in the attic. I still hadn't told her about the pages. When I heard her walk to the far end of the house, I dropped the ladder and nearly slid down the steps. I'm pretty sure my stealthy attempt would have worked had I not bellowed, "OUCH," when a giant splinter made it's way under the skin of my index finger. As if I'd lost an arm or a leg, Mom's socked feet skidded around the corner in true heroine fashion.

"What? What is it? What happened?" I held up my finger. "Savannah, you nearly scared me to death!" Mom looked at the ladder that was hanging halfway from the ceiling.

Oops, I thought.

"Honey, why is the ladder down? Were you in the attic?"

I stood there hoping she wasn't going to ask me why. "Yes." *Think quickly, Savannah.* "I, um, I was doing some research for my science class. We're studying mice, and I thought I might find one in the attic."

My mom looked at me with the most blank and confused stare. "Well, let's hope not," she said, shaking her head and reaching for my finger. "That splinter is pretty deep. I'll go get the tweezers."

"No," I replied briskly. "It's fine. I'll get it out."

"Are you sure, honey? It will only take a second."

The only thing on my mind at that moment was getting back to the pages I had dropped when Mom called for me. "I'm sure."

"Oh, I almost forgot. Your school called. All of the classrooms that were affected by the kitchen fire have been ventilated, and classes will start at the normal time tomorrow. So don't stay up too late, okay?"

Reluctantly, I agreed. I knew there was at least another chapter in the attic and maybe even two. Mom headed back down the hall, and I pulled the ladder from the ceiling. *I'll have to read quickly*, I thought as I gathered the pages. I leaned my back against the trunk and found my place in the story.

The Heist

"Buddy!" yelled Milo. "Where are you going? Come back. Buddy, no! Buddy! Buddy!" Milo yelled and yelled, but Buddy was gone in a flash. He took off as if he were in a race and the prize was a lifetime supply of treat biscuits. It wasn't like Buddy to disobey Milo. Buddy took his status as man's best friend very seriously. He always stayed by Milo's side. He was the picture-perfect dog – loyal, obedient, smart, and super-intuitive. Milo rarely needed to give Buddy a command because Buddy would always beat him to it. It was as if Buddy had a sixth sense for what Milo wanted. Buddy prided himself on being perfect.

"Great, now I just look stupid," muttered Buddy under his breath as he ran away from Milo. "Here I am running away from my human like some untrained, common mutt. This is so not me!"

Buddy raced toward Milo's farm. He knew he would need Tyne E.'s help to unlock the doors on Ol' Betsy, and his time was limited. He ran as fast as his paws would carry him.

"Tyne E.!" Buddy barked loudly as he rushed into the barn.

"Aaaoooaaahhh," Tyne E. yawned as he crawled out from under a pile of hay stashed in the corner of P's stall. "Isn't it a little early for you to be back? I haven't even finished my afternoon nap."

"Never mind your nap, we've got bigger problems," Buddy said.

Tyne E. stretched his little mouse arms high above his head. "This better be good," he said. "I was having the best dream. P and I were running in the Kentucky Derby, and the track was made of peanut butter."

"Tyne E., this is serious." Buddy tried to catch his breath. "Milo has a picture of you riding P, and he's going to show it to all of his friends at Eastwood. The picture is in Ol' Betsy, and the doors are locked. You're the only one small enough to squeeze through a crack and get inside. We only have a little time to get back there, so we have to hurry."

Tyne E. hopped on Buddy's back with no time to waste. "Come on, Bird. We may need your help," Tyne E. yelled as Buddy took off running.

Doc waved as many of his arms as he could lift off the ground at once. "Wait! If Bird goes, I go. Bird is my assistant, and I must be there to oversee the events that take place. Plus, I am an expert at just about everything, so I am quite certain that my presence will be needed. In fact, I don't believe you three can pull this off without me. Pick me up, Bird. Let's go." As Bird flew away carrying Doc in his beak, Doc shouted to P, "No worries, Zebra! I've got this under control!"

The foursome rushed to Eastwood stables to pull off the big heist and defend their friend. When they arrived, Doc, in his own brilliant fashion, began to orchestrate a plan.

"Little mouse," Doc said to Tyne E., "you will go find a small piece of metal. Bird, you will use your beak to grind a key out of it. Dog, you will jump up on the door and…"

Before Doc could finish unveiling his grand plan, Tyne E. had already squeezed through a small hole in the floorboard of Ol' Betsy and unlocked the door. "Okay, it's unlocked!" Tyne E. yelled from inside the truck. "Now, how are we going to get this door open? It's too heavy for me."

"You must have read my mind," said Doc to Tyne E. "I knew it would work! All you had to do was squeeze through that hole in the floorboard. That was my original idea."

While Doc patted himself on the back and basked in his self-proclaimed glory, Buddy decided to find a piece of bailing twine and tie it to the door handle of Ol' Betsy. Tyne E. squeezed back out of the truck and helped Buddy thread the twine through the handle. Then they tied a knot with the loose ends and pulled it tight.

"Bird," said Buddy, "I need you to use your beak to press against the button on the door handle. While you press the button, I will pull back against the twine and the door should open.

"Wait!" shouted Doc. "Let me see here. Hmmm, Bird presses the button; you pull the handle. Yes, yes. That should work splendidly. Carry on. Carry on."

So Buddy began to pull the twine as Bird pressed against the button on the door handle with all of his might.

CREEEEEK! The door began to open.

"Pull, Buddy! Pull!" shouted Tyne E. Buddy pulled as hard as he could until the door finally swung open. Bird flapped and fluttered his wings in excitement.

"Victory, my friends, victory!" declared Doc with pride.

"Tyne E., you get the picture and stuff it under my bandanna," said Buddy. "We'll hide it somewhere safe when we get home."

So Tyne E. rummaged through Milo's coat pockets until he found the picture. While Bird lifted Buddy's bandanna, Tyne E. crawled under it and tucked the picture securely beneath Buddy's collar.

"Done!" said Tyne E. as he jumped down to the ground.

"Good job, fellas!" said Buddy with pride. "Bird, can you fly Doc home?" asked Buddy. "Tyne E. and I will be right behind you. We'll figure out what to do with this picture tonight after feeding time. Meet me in the barn after sunset."

Bird nodded his head in agreement and flew off with Doc in his beak, while Tyne E. crawled back in Ol' Betsy and waited for Buddy and Milo.

"Now, I have to figure out how to redeem myself," Buddy muttered under his breath as he headed toward the stables. "I know: I'll do the old sticker in the paw trick! It gets sympathy every time. No one can be mad at a limping dog."

"Buddy!" Milo yelled as he saw his dog in the distance. "Where have you been, boy? You know better than to run off like that, boy. You could have gotten lost or been hit by a car. I've been looking for you all afternoon. Bad dog. Bad…wait, are you limping? Are you hurt? Oh poor pup, let me take a look."

Buddy eased toward Milo, limping as pitifully as he could. When he reached Milo, he sat down and began licking his right front paw.

"Aw Buddy, you hurt your paw. Let's see," said Milo as he knelt down beside Buddy and held out his hand. Buddy lifted his paw as if he were shaking Milo's hand. Milo took Buddy's paw, and in that moment Buddy knew all was forgiven.

"That's what happens when you run off," said Milo. "You'll need to rest it for a couple of days, and you'll be good as new in no time. Now, let's go home and get you some treat biscuits."

With Buddy by his side, Milo headed toward the truck. When they got there, Milo opened the door and grabbed his jacket from the seat.

"I've got to find my picture to show the guys, and then we're headed home," Milo said to Buddy. Milo checked both pockets of his jacket but did not find his picture. "I know it was here. Maybe it fell out on the seat." He looked all around the truck, but there was no sign of his picture. "I don't believe it. That was the only picture I had, and now it's gone." Buddy sat proudly in the front seat of Ol' Betsy with Milo's picture well hidden beneath his bandanna.

Milo drove home and gave Buddy his extra treat biscuits as promised. After sunset, when a cloak of darkness covered the farm, Buddy sneaked out into the barn and met his friends.

"Okay fellas," Buddy announced, "it's our duty to make sure this picture remains unseen by Milo or any of his human friends. We need a hiding place, and I'm open to suggestions."

"No worries, Buddy," replied Tyne E. "This is a hay barn, is it not?"

"Yes," answered Buddy.

"So we will hide it in the hay," said Tyne E. "I can bury it underneath all these bales. Milo will never find it. I'll make a path to the middle of the stack and tuck it into the center bale."

"Perfect!" replied Buddy.

"Nom crunch nom crunch. I could just eat the picture," said P as he chewed his dinner hay.

"Zebras don't eat photo paper," replied Doc. "Tyne E., before you hide the picture, you must shred it. You always destroy the evidence. Don't you novices know anything? Oh! What would you all do without me!" declared Doc. "Bird, I'm ready to retire for the evening."

While Bird flew Doc to his home above P's stall door, Buddy and Tyne E. considered Doc's suggestion and agreed that shredding the picture before burying it in the hay was the best thing to do. Together, Buddy and Tyne E. tore the picture in half and then tore those halves in half again. That night, Tyne E. took the four ripped and tattered pieces of what had been a marvelous picture to the center of Milo's stock of hay.

The plan worked splendidly. Buddy and Tyne E., with the help of their friends, had saved P from a fate of certain misery under the ownership of old mean Mr. Cheatham – or so they thought.

You see, the crew's plan would have worked perfectly had it not been for Milo's untimely decision to sell half of his hay stock to a buyer who had offered top dollar for high quality, fresh hay. Milo grew some of the best hay in the state. He had inherited ten acres of farmland from his grandparents. Every year, Milo farmed the land so that he could grow hay for the local stables. Each summer Milo harvested his crop of hay and sold it throughout the year to make extra money, but this year was different. Instead of selling to a lot of small buyers, Milo got a very large order from one buyer. Milo was not about to pass up such a great opportunity to sell his yearly quota of hay, so he told the man he could pick up his bales the very next day.

Buddy was napping inside on the couch when a large, black dually pulled into the driveway towing a long, flatbed trailer. The truck backed the trailer up to the doors of the hay barn and the driver began loading the hay. P was at the far end of the pasture, grazing, while Tyne E. rummaged through Milo's cupboards for tasty crumbs. Bird, who never left his perch without the company of his companion and chief officer Doc, was freshening up in the birdbath in the front yard.

"My dogs are barkin'!" Doc said to Bird as he soaked his many feet in the birdbath. "After I wash my feet, I'm going to put these puppies up!"

Completely clueless, the crew of friends happily carried on with their daily activities while, bale by bale, the stack dwindled. Each bale loaded was one bale closer to the remnants of the freshly buried picture. When the driver was done loading the hay, he left a check on Milo's doorstep. The sound of unusual footsteps outside the front door woke Buddy from his nap, and he hopped off the couch to investigate. As Buddy pushed his way through the doggie door, he saw the taillights of the truck pulling out of Milo's long driveway. Buddy looked down and saw the check the man had left for Milo. In the top left corner of the check, Buddy saw the words *Cheatham Racing Stables*.

Buddy couldn't believe what he was seeing. The check to pay for the hay was written by old Mr. Cheatham! Buddy immediately headed for the barn to see if the picture was still hidden. When he got there, he saw nearly all of the hay had been hauled away. There was no sign of the picture.

"Where's the hay?" Tyne E. shouted as he ran into the barn with P following just moments behind him.

Buddy hated to break the news to Tyne E., and especially to P, but he knew the damage had already been done. The picture was gone, and there was nothing any of them could do about it now.

"Cheatham," mumbled Buddy with his head low to the ground. "Cheatham bought the hay. And that means he also has the picture." Buddy could barely look at P as he told them about finding the check and seeing the taillights of Cheatham's truck as he drove away with the hay.

The crew knew the missing picture was a ticking time bomb. At any moment, old mean Mr. Cheatham could find the picture, trace it back to Milo's farm, and find P.

Chapter Nine

The All-nighter

Mom's request that I not stay up late left my mind just as quickly as I made my decision to read another chapter. After all, there was only one more left, and Mom had said for me not to stay up *too* late. I understood that my definition of *too* late and her definition of *too* late were most likely not the same. But had she wanted me in bed at a certain time, she would have said, "Savannah, be in bed by ten." She hadn't said that, so with a somewhat clear conscience I decided reading that last chapter was just the thing to do, even if it meant puffy eyes and a yawning marathon awaited me Wednesday morning.

The Hind End

Months passed, and the crew of friends had all but forgotten about the lost picture. The hay in Cheatham's barn dwindled. Layer after layer of hay was used with no sign of the picture. With months of worry behind them, Buddy and Tyne E. finally assumed the picture would never be found. And it might not have, had it not been for the annual spring-cleaning of Mr. Cheatham's stables.

Every year, after the pollen fell, Mr. Cheatham held his annual barn cleaning and tack sale event. All of the small-time trainers, jockey hopefuls, and local racing fans looked forward to the event each spring. Mr. Cheatham was known to have only the finest racing tack and training tools, and he liked to replace his bridles, bits, and saddles every year with the latest and greatest new editions. A lot of the tack sold at Cheatham's annual event was barely used and like brand new, making the sale a horseman's toy store. Cheatham even had activities for the kids who came to the sale with their parents. As a shrewd businessman, he knew keeping the youngsters busy meant more shopping time for the parents. More shopping meant more cash in old man Cheatham's pockets, so every year he had bouncy houses, cotton candy machines, and games for the kids to play. It was an event any horseman would love, and Milo was no exception. He never missed one of Cheatham's tack sales.

This year was no different than any other. The turnout was great as usual. The weather was superb, and Cheatham had plenty of tack to sell. There was money to be made, and that meant old man Cheatham was in the thick of the action. From the arrival of the first customer to the departure of the last, Mr. Cheatham wandered through the crowd: cutting deals, making sales, and overseeing the event. He always liked to keep an eye on the merchandise – and on his employees. He was known as a pill to work for – grouchy, impatient, and worst of all, stingy.

Milo had been at the sale for only ten minutes when he saw Mr. Cheatham barreling toward him with a small piece of paper in his right hand.

"Morning, sir," said Milo with a smile. "How's that hay working out for you? It was a great crop this year."

"Cut the small talk, kid," snapped Cheatham. "This picture was just given to me by those pesky little boys over there." Cheatham pointed toward three boys, probably around the age of ten, who were being scolded by their mother. "I just ran them out of my hay barn. The little nuisances were climbing on the bales. All I need is for one of those little brats to fall, break his leg, and his parents sue me!"

Mr. Cheatham held up a picture in front of Milo's face and said angrily, "Those boys claim they found this picture in the hay. Now, I'm no detective, but I know one of my horses when I see it, and that's Pumpernickel and

Mayo's hind end. Where's my horse, boy?" Old man Cheatham angrily shook his finger at Milo.

"Sir, I'm sorry to say I don't know what you're talking about," replied Milo.

"Look, just look at the picture," shouted Mr. Cheatham as he handed the torn piece of photo paper to Milo.

Milo looked at the paper and saw that it was a piece of the picture he had taken months before. The picture was torn and hard to make out, but anyone who knew P knew he had a distinct marking near the top of his left hip. It was very noticeable, like a birthmark.

"Yeah, that's my horse!" said Milo proudly. "I've been looking for this picture. It must have somehow ended up in the hay I sold you. I wish you had found the other pieces, too. It's a picture of a mou…"

Mr. Cheatham interrupted him. "You stay right here. Don't you move a muscle. I'm going to get

Pumpernickel and Mayo's registration papers. Then you're going to take me to my horse."

When Mr. Cheatham came back with the papers, he explained to Milo how his racehorse, Pumpernickel and Mayo, had run away the previous winter during a training exercise. He had jumped the fence at the track and was never found – until today. Milo's heart sank as he realized the horse he had cared for and grown to love would soon have to leave his farm.

"Mr. Cheatham, sir, this is an innocent mistake. I had no idea he was your horse. The first time I saw him, he was walking down the road near my farm. He was covered in cuts and scratches and was limping as though he'd hurt his hoof. I stopped my truck and got out to help him, but he got spooked and ran off into the woods. The next morning I found him in my barn. I've taken care of him ever since," said Milo.

"Maybe if you'd left him alone, he would have come home," spouted Mr. Cheatham in a snarky voice.

Now, most people would have thanked Milo at this point and may have even offered him a reward for finding their horse, but they didn't call Mr. Cheatham old mean Cheatham for nothing.

"Is there any way we can work something out, sir?" pleaded Milo. "I've grown so attached to him. He's a great horse. Would you be willing to let me buy him from you?"

"Kid, first of all, he's not a great horse. He's scared of his own shadow. But he is fast, and fast is all that matters in my business. I can get a scared horse to run. A little discipline with a horse like Pumpernickel and Mayo will go a long way. He can either be scared of the track or scared of my whip, but one way or another, he'll run. If you want him, you'll have to pay top dollar."

"How much do you want for him?" asked Milo.

Mr. Cheatham looked toward the ground as he rubbed the toe of his boot in the dirt. When he looked up at Milo, he replied, "Ten grand."

"Ten thousand dollars," said Milo in disbelief. Milo had known the price would not be cheap, but he hadn't expected it to be so steep either. "I don't have that much money. Could I possibly work it off? I could work in your stables every weekend until you're paid in full."

"Boy, it would take you a lifetime of weekends to make that much money. Besides, I deal in cash. I don't barter, and I don't do favors," said Mr. Cheatham. "Now you had best take me to my horse."

Heartbroken, Milo spent the whole ride back to his farm swallowing the huge lump in his throat. When Milo pulled into the driveway, Buddy immediately noticed something was amiss. He saw a big, black dually pulling a silver horse trailer following behind Milo's truck. As the dually got closer, Buddy read the words painted on the side of the truck door. They were the same words he had seen months before: *Cheatham Racing Stables*.

Buddy ran straight to the barn to warn P, but there simply wasn't enough time. Mr. Cheatham got out of his truck with a halter in his hand and walked into Milo's barn. When P saw Mr. Cheatham, he began to snort furiously and stomp his hooves into the packed-dirt floor of his stall.

"Settle down, horse!" yelled Cheatham as he opened the stall door.

Buddy growled and bit the leg of Mr. Cheatham's pants, tugging at it with all his might.

"Buddy!" yelled Milo. "Down boy!" He ran over to Buddy and grabbed him by the collar.

"He never acts like this toward people," Milo said to Mr. Cheatham.

"Just keep your dog out of my way, so I can halter this horse," snapped Mr. Cheatham.

On Mr. Cheatham's second attempt to open the stall door, P once again snorted and stomped. Cheatham opened the door only a little and squeezed through, swinging the halter toward P.

"Back up! Back! Get back!" yelled Cheatham, but the more Mr. Cheatham yelled at P, the more scared P became.

"Maybe I should get him for you," suggested Milo, as he struggled to hold Buddy back.

"He's my horse. I'll do it," huffed Cheatham.

"He may be your horse, sir," replied Milo, "but this is my dog, and I can't hold him back forever."

Frustrated and out of breath, mean old Mr. Cheatham finally agreed to let Milo halter P so they could get him into the horse trailer. And just like that, P was gone. Buddy watched helplessly as the trailer carrying his friend pulled away. Mr. Cheatham rolled down his window and yelled at Milo as he left, "Remember, ten thousand dollars and he's yours. Fast horses don't come free, boy."

When the dust settled, Buddy walked into P's stall and lay down.

"You don't look well," said Doc to Buddy. Doc had witnessed the whole event perched atop P's stall door. "Let me examine you to make sure you weren't hurt in the scuffle."

Bird flew Doc down to the ground and placed him on a blade of hay next to Buddy. "Your ankle looks a little puffy," said Doc. "Can you bend it?"

"Yes," answered Buddy. "I'm fine, Doc. I don't need an examination."

"Nonsense. I am a professional, so this will only take a moment. Bird is going to perform a simple test on your ankle to see if it is broken," replied Doc. "Now, perform the test, Bird."

Bird hopped over to Buddy and quickly poked Buddy's ankle with his beak.

"Ouch!"

"Splendid!" declared Doc. "I have great news. Your ankle is not broken."

"How do you know?" asked Buddy.

"Because if it were, you would have barked louder," answered Doc in the most certain of tones.

"Well thanks, Doc." Buddy wrinkled his brow. "I think."

"What you need is good old-fashioned ice therapy. I want you to take two ice cubes, and call me in the morning," instructed Doc.

Chapter Ten

Only One Mouse

When my alarm interrupted the rhythmic thiththiththiththiththith sound of my ceiling fan cutting through the air in my room, I awoke with one thought – *today I confront Mr. Weiss*. The morning was like any other with one exception, I was emboldened. The more of Granddad's story I read, the more certain I was of my unwillingness to dissect anything, let alone a mouse. Every time I thought of that small, innocent mouse, I envisioned Tyne E. and his friends.

I walked through the tall doors of Ward Middle that Wednesday morning feeling like an unstoppable force for good. I didn't know what was going to happen in the rest of Granddad's story. I didn't know if P would ever see his friends again or if Tyne E. would ever fulfill his dream of becoming a jockey. But what I did know, what I knew with absolute certainty, was the mouse designated to Savannah Ashford for dissection would not meet the fate Mr. Weiss had assigned.

"Mr. Weiss, I need to speak with you." A polite request, or at least so I thought.

"Savannah," Mr. Weiss replied glancing up from a stack of papers he had been grading while his homeroom students took their seats before the first bell. "Savannah, this isn't your homeroom." Mr. Weiss continued grading his papers, showing what I perceived as less respect than I had given him. I mean, I could have just bellowed out my intentions to never, under any circumstances, participate in his horrid, cruel assignment. But I didn't do that. I requested to speak with him as any well-mannered student would, and for that I expected courteous attentiveness. I had to up the ante.

"Mr. Weiss, I need to speak with you about a very serious subject, and I would appreciate your full attention." He stopped grading. An expression came over his face that I had never seen during any of his biology lectures.

"Oookay," he replied in a tone that seemed to me more cautious than curious. I was not one to speak up often in class, nor had I ever spoken to Mr. Weiss outside of fifth period. "I'm all ears, Miss Ashford."

I swallowed the knot that had spontaneously formed in my throat and wiped my clammy hands on the sides of my blue jeans. "Well, first of all, I just want to say that I've given this a lot of thought, Mr. Weiss. And my decision is final." I paused.

"Yes, Savannah?" He waited.

"I can't dissect a mouse. I'm sorry Mr. Weiss, but I just can't. I won't."

"I see," Mr. Weiss replied as he scratched the red whiskers that made up his patchy beard. "And how do you suggest I calculate your grade? This project is weighted as heavily as a final. An incomplete would drop your grade for the quarter to..." Mr. Weiss picked up his faux leather grade book. "Well, wait just a moment and I'll tell you." He licked his thumb and began flipping through the pages briskly, as if he were counting money. "Ah, there you are, Miss Savannah Ashford." His finger glided across the page and over my grades. My fate resided on that page: a compiled grade system supposedly representing my knowledge of the information presented to me that entire quarter. But as Mr. Weiss tapped the touch screen of his phone, adding and dividing my numerical academic fate, I felt compelled to interrupt.

"I don't care," I asserted with enough volume to even surprise myself. Mr. Weiss stopped his page flipping and his number tapping.

"Excuse me, Savannah?"

"I said I don't care what my grade will be if I don't complete the project."

"Savannah, this is very out of character for you. May I ask why you are so adamant? It's only one mouse. It's not worth failing my class and having to repeat it next year."

Only one mouse, only one mouse. Tell that to Tyne E. Tell that to P and Buddy. Tell that to my grandfather who obviously thought enough of one mouse to write an entire story about him. For me, every mouse represented Tyne E., and as long as I had Tyne E., I had my granddad.

"Mr. Weiss, I don't care if I fail." I fixed my backpack strap higher on my shoulder, planted my feet, raised my chin, and crossed my skinny arms. Mr. Weiss sucked in a deep breath then forcefully huffed it from his lungs. I could tell he was perturbed, but I stood firm.

"I'll tell you what, Savannah. I'll give you an alternate assignment, but you have to turn it in, completed, by Friday morning." My stance softened at his words, my arms relaxed a bit, and I may have even mustered a slight smile. Then he continued, "I want you to write a paper convincing me why one mouse is so important. Now don't think this will be easy. You can't just write about how you refuse to participate in my dissection assignment because you don't *want* to dissect a mouse. You have to convince me, and I mean *really* convince me, that this one mouse is worth more than your grade in my class. If it truly means that much to you, Savannah, you shouldn't have a problem writing a persuasive paper and changing my mind. When you turn in the paper Friday morning, I'll read it, and then I'll make my decision about whether or not you have to participate in the dissection project." Mr. Weiss raised his right eyebrow, the one that was always disheveled from him resting his index finger against it. "Does that sound fair to you?"

Fair? Fair is subjective, I thought. *Fair isn't one mouse getting sent to an unfortunate demise so a student can pass biology. Fair isn't P getting sent back to Mr. Cheatham's to face unthinkable treatment. Fair isn't Tyne E. being left without his new friend and losing his dream of becoming a real jockey.* But, fair *is* what Mr. Weiss had proposed. He had given me an out, an opportunity to boycott mouse dissection while still earning a passing grade. And that was all I needed. I was happy.

When I got home from school that afternoon, I went straight to my room to begin writing my project. I threw my backpack on the floor beside my clothes from the day before and ripped two pieces of paper from the doodle pad I kept on the corner of my desk. I grabbed my favorite fat, purple pen with the pink feather decoration on top and began to brainstorm. How could I convince Mr. Weiss that my mouse was worth saving? I tapped my pen against my thigh and bobbed my heel up and down in a quick, nervous twitch. That usually helped me during the thinking process. When that didn't work as it normally did, I resorted to chewing my thumbnails, first my right hand, then my left. When nothing, not one idea, entered my brain after a good two hours of gnawing, I knew I was in trouble. There was only one thing to do – retreat. So that is exactly what I did. I tiptoed down the hall and lowered the attic ladder for the fourth night in a row. I may not have been able to write anything that night, but I definitely had something to read. When I opened the trunk, I found another set of pages, and I let myself escape into the world my granddad was sharing with me.

Peanut Butter and Anything with Pickle on Top

Buddy lay in P's stall the rest of the day, thinking of how he was going to break the news to Tyne E. that P had been found and taken back to old mean Mr. Cheatham's farm. Tyne E. had spent the weekend at Eastwood Stables with his family, so that night Buddy sneaked out and made the trip to Eastwood. When he arrived, the barn was quiet. The hustle and bustle of pounding hooves; rickety, squeaking hay carts; and all of the usual noises Buddy had been accustomed to hearing at the stables during the day were not present at night. Much to Buddy's surprise, Eastwood Stables was rather peaceful without jockeys, trainers, and farm hands.

"Tyne E.," Buddy whispered. Buddy knew Tyne E. lived in Barn Fifteen, but he had never been to Tyne E.'s burrow, and for obvious reasons he was hesitant to barge in on Tyne E.'s family without notice. A dog-and-mouse friendship wasn't typical, and the last thing Buddy wanted to do was scare Tyne E.'s family.

"Tyne E.," Buddy whispered again. "It's me, Buddy."

Suddenly, Buddy heard the shrill squeaks of a mouse as it scurried along the side of the barn.

Meanwhile Tyne E., along with Mr. and Mrs. Tells, Tall, and Harry, had just sat down at the dinner table when they heard the alarm sound.

"Dog, dog, there is a dog in the barn!" squeaked the mouse stationed at the neighborhood guard gate. "Everyone into your burrows!"

"No, no," said Buddy. "I'm only looking for my friend. Perhaps you could direct me to the Tells' residence." But the mouse was gone before Buddy could even finish his sentence.

The warning echoed through all of the burrows as each mouse family spread the word to their neighbors to stay in their homes because a dog was on the loose. It only took minutes for word to travel to Tyne E.'s burrow. As soon as it did, Tyne E. jumped up from the table and ran straight toward the door.

"Tyne E., just where do you think you're going?" asked Mrs. Tells.

"I think I might have a visitor," answered Tyne E.

"Tyne E., a dog alert has just been issued. This is no time for visitors!"

"Yes, but I think the dog is my visitor," said Tyne E. "I'll be right back. Don't worry; I know what I'm doing. I know every nook and cranny in this barn. I won't get caught." Tyne E. hurried through the door of the burrow and closed it behind him.

Tyne E. ran quietly alongside the tall stack of hay that sat in front of their burrow door until he reached the corner of the barn where the tractor was parked. He climbed onto the bucket of the tractor and ran up into the seat and onto the steering wheel so he could get a better look. When he reached the top, Tyne E. saw Buddy sniffing around the opposite corner of the barn.

"If you're looking for treat biscuits, you've come to the wrong place. But I could make you one of my signature peanut butter and pickle sandwiches," Tyne E. yelled across the barn.

"There you are!" said Buddy. "I thought I'd never find you. I ran into one of your pals, and he wasn't too helpful."

"Yeah," replied Tyne E. "That was probably the night patrol you ran into. They're usually the only ones out this time of night. Well, come on and follow me. I want you to meet my family."

"Actually, I need to talk to you," said Buddy.

Tyne E. didn't hear him. He was so excited for Buddy to meet his family that he took off toward his burrow, paying no mind to Buddy's request.

Knock, knock, knock. "Mom, let me in. There's someone I want you to meet," said Tyne E. Mrs. Tells had been guarding the door awaiting her son's return. When she opened it, she saw Tyne E. standing there proudly with a large, wet, dog nose directly behind him.

"Oh my," gasped Mrs. Tells. "Tyne E., whatever you do, don't look behind you."

"Mom, I know what's behind me." Tyne E. laughed. "Trust me, he's nothing to be scared of. This is Buddy. He's a friend of mine."

Mr. Tells promptly jumped up from the table to introduce himself and calm his clearly startled wife.

"Now now, dear," Mr. Tells whispered in his wife's ear as he patted her shoulders, "let's show our guest some Tells family hospitality."

"Any friend of Tyne E.'s is a friend of ours," Mr. Tells declared loudly. "I would invite you inside, but it appears your nose is as far you would get. At any rate, your nose is welcome to come in and join us!" Mr. Tells laughed. He always thought his jokes were funnier than they actually were. He turned to his other sons. "Boys, perhaps you could share a portion of your dinner with our guest."

"Sure," said Harry, who laid a piece of cheese in front of Buddy's nose.

"You can have my peanut butter sandwich," said Tyne E.

"And what about you, Tall?" Mr. Tells asked as he watched his oldest son, the lawyer, scribble furiously on a piece of paper.

Tall answered, "Buddy, you can have a one quarter portion of my cheese; but before I proceed in the exchange of said goods, you must sign here please."

"What is this?" Buddy asked as he sniffed the paper.

"It's a hold-harmless agreement, in case you choke on a scrumptious morsel of my food. One can never be too careful," said Tall.

Buddy tapped the paper with his nose to make his signature, and chowed down on the delicious meal Mrs. Tells had prepared.

"This is really good." Buddy smacked his lips as he licked the excess peanut butter from all around his mouth. "What is this again?"

"It's peanut butter," replied Tyne E. "You mean to tell me you've never tasted peanut butter? Why, it's only the best food on earth – savory and sweet, creamy and crunchy! I eat it every day. Peanut butter makes all the best sandwiches – peanut butter and pickles, peanut butter and banana, peanut butter and chocolate, peanut butter and marshmallows, peanut butter and jelly, peanut butter and honey, peanut butter and bacon, peanut butter and potato chip…"

"Ahem." Knowing from past experience that Tyne E.'s list could go on forever, Mrs. Tells politely interrupted. "Who would like dessert? I have crumb cake."

Mrs. Tells made the best crumb cake in the neighborhood, and it was true to its name because it indeed was made entirely of crumbs. Every day, after the barn hands finished their lunches, Mrs. Tells made a trip to the break room to gather up all of the leftover snack-cake crumbs. Her exact recipe was a family secret, but her favorite ingredient was not.

"You all are going to love this one!" said Mrs. Tells. "It's full of zebra cake!"

"Sounds great, Mom," said Tyne E. He turned to Buddy. "Speaking of zebras, how's my pal P?"

"Well actually, that's why I'm here," answered Buddy. "Tyne E., I don't know how to tell you this, so I'll just give it to you straight. Mr. Cheatham came this morning and hauled P away. I did everything I could to stop him."

"What?" gasped Tyne E. "Where is P now? We have to go find him. Come on, Buddy, we don't have time to waste!"

"Tyne E., we can't just go get him. It's more complicated than that. It turns out that Cheatham is P's rightful owner. Even if we broke him out and brought him home, Cheatham would just come back and take him again. The only way to bring P home for good is for Milo to buy him from Mr. Cheatham, and the price is steep," said Buddy.

"How much?" asked Tyne E.

"Ten thousand dollars," replied Buddy. "And Milo doesn't have it."

"So we'll get it," said Tyne E.

"Where are we going to get ten thousand dollars?" asked Buddy.

"Ahem," interrupted Tall as he cleared his throat. "Look guys, I think it's time you two get some professional advice. My fee is one hundred and fifty dollars an hour plus an upfront retainer of one thousand dollars. Since you are family, I will give you a ten percent discount which I will have to waive because you are family."

Tyne E. wrinkled his brow and replied, "Tall, that makes no sense."

"Which part?" asked Tall as he pushed a piece of paper toward Tyne E. and Buddy. "Sign here. It's an agreement for my services."

"Tall Ferry Tells!" scolded Mrs. Tells as she picked up the paper. "Tyne E. is your little brother. You will help him or that will be the last piece of crumb cake you'll ever see!"

"Mom, you know I hate it when you call me by my middle name," whispered Tall. He then turned to Tyne E. and said, "Fine, I'll waive my usual fees. But I call dibs on your piece of crumb cake."

"Deal," replied Tyne E. He pushed his piece of crumb cake across the table toward his brother.

Chomping down on his second piece of cake, Tall began to unveil his plan.

"Your friend, P," said Tall, "is he fast?"

"Very," replied Tyne E.

"Then you need to race him," said Tall. "You said you needed ten thousand dollars. The Palmetto Derby Race is coming up at Eastwood Stables in just two short weeks. All of the local racehorses run in it, so I'm sure Mr. Cheatham will have P there. The purse is ten grand. All you need to do is enter P into the race as Milo's horse, let him run, and then claim the prize."

"But how are we going to enter P into the race as Milo's? He's registered to Mr. Cheatham," said Buddy. "When Cheatham came to pick him up, he had the papers in his hand – Pumpernickel and Mayo registered to L.D. Cheatham III."

"Pumpernickel and Mayo?" said Tyne E. "So that's his full name. I always wondered what the P stood for. Personally, I think Peanut Butter and, well, Peanut Butter and anything would have suited him better than Pumpernickel and Mayo."

"Well, there's your answer," said Tall. "Don't race Pumpernickel and Mayo, race Peanut Butter and Anything."

"What?" said Tyne E., a bit confused at his brother's proposition.

"What does P look like?" asked Tall.

"He's a black and white Paint," replied Tyne E.

"Perfect!" said Tall. He turned to his brother. "Harry, we may need your help with this one. We need you to turn P into a solid black Thoroughbred."

"No problem," replied Harry. "I'll give him the full makeover – shampoo, cut, and color. He'll look like the Black Stallion by the time I'm done with him."

"Now, Tyne E., you will need to register P as Peanut Butter and Anything, with Milo listed as his owner, at the racing secretary's office before the race. I will prepare the paperwork, but you will have to make sure it gets on the secretary's desk before the race," Tall said.

"It's as good as done," replied Tyne E. "Tall, I think your plan just might be the answer to our problems. Now all I have to do is get P ready. And I only have two weeks!"

"Why wouldn't he be ready?" asked Tall. "You said he was fast. I thought he was supposed to be an excellent racehorse. You know this plan will only work if he wins the race, and to win the race, he has to be ready."

"I know, I know," said Tyne E. "He'll be ready. And he is fast. He just doesn't exactly embrace the essence of a fearless, stampeding warrior. He's not your typical racehorse. P can be, ummm, a little unpredictable."

"What are you trying to say, Tyne E.?" asked Tall.

"Well," said Tyne E. hesitantly. "P has a bit of an amnesia problem, and sometimes that makes it hard for him to race. That's how he ended up at Milo's farm in the first place. One of old mean Cheatham's jockeys was racing P on the training track, something spooked P, and the rest is history. He jumped over the guardrail and took off into the woods. Milo and Buddy found him wandering down the road later that same day. Poor P couldn't even remember his own name. All he knew was that it started with a P. But don't worry. He'll be able to race come Derby day. I'll figure something out. The amnesia only kicks in when P's scared. I just have to make sure nothing scares him during the race, and that ten thousand dollar purse is as good as ours."

That night after dinner, Tyne E. left his family at Eastwood Stables and traveled back to Milo's farm to tell the rest of the crew about his plan to save P. By the time Buddy and Tyne E. reached Milo's farm, it was well past Doc and Bird's bedtime. When Buddy walked into the barn with Tyne E. riding atop his neck, the two saw Bird snoozing peacefully in his nest and Doc stretched across the top of the stall door talking in his sleep.

"I am the greatest," mumbled Doc as he slept. "I am a champion. I am a world-renowned doctor, the greatest in my profession. I am beautiful and have more legs than any caterpillar around. Chicks dig me. Yes, you can have my autograph…"

"Ok, that's enough. I don't think I can listen to anymore of that. Wake up, Doc!" shouted Buddy.

"Wha – what? Is it time to get up already? Oh, it's too early, and Bird hasn't made my latte yet," said Doc sleepily.

"No," replied Buddy. "It's the middle of the night."

"Then why in the world would you wake me? Haven't you ever heard the old saying about never waking a sleeping caterpillar?"

"I can't say I have," replied Buddy. "We woke you because we need to talk to you and Bird about P."

"We have a plan to get him back from Cheatham's," said Tyne E.

Unable to sleep through the racket, Bird began to stir about in his nest.

"Come down and join us, Bird," said Tyne E. "I'm going to need your help for this plan to work."

Bird fluttered down to the ground, and Tyne E. revealed his plan step by step to Doc and Bird. He asked for Bird's help delivering the paperwork to the racing secretary's office once Tall had everything ready. Eager to help, Bird nodded his head, and the crew agreed that the plan was perfect, except for one minor detail.

"You need a nickname," said Doc to Tyne E.

"What? Why would I need a nickname?" asked Tyne E.

"All the great athletes have them. If you're going to be P's jockey, excuse me, Peanut Butter and Anything's jockey, then you need a nickname."

"I don't think that'll be necessary," said Tyne E. "I'm not really a nickname kind of guy."

"Pickle," said Doc. "You'll be Pickle."

"Pickle?" asked Tyne E. in a disapproving voice. "I don't think so, Doc."

"Oh yes," insisted Doc. "I can hear the announcer now. '*Here comes Peanut Butter and Anything rounding the corner. Peanut Butter and Anything with Pickle on top is taking the lead. Wait, did the jockey fall off? Peanut Butter and Anything, hold the Pickle? No, I think I see him. Yes, he's still there. He's hanging on to the saddle. Peanut Butter and*

Anything with Pickle on the side wins by a nose!' I can hear the crowds cheering now!" Doc chuckled.

"Okay, Doc," said Tyne E. "You can give the Pickle thing a rest. I don't need a nickname."

"Well, all right," replied Doc. "If you don't want a nickname, that's fine. I'll just call you Tyne E."

"Thanks," said Tyne E.

"But I still want you to *relish* this opportunity." Doc laughed.

"Real funny," replied Tyne E. "Bird, I don't know how you put up with him." Tyne E. shook his head and winked at Bird.

"Well guys, there is still someone else we need to tell about this plan, and I'm not sure how we are going to do it," said Buddy. "One of us has to find a way to get word to P about the race."

"That would be easier if we knew exactly where he was," replied Tyne E. "We need old man Cheatham's address."

"Good point," said Buddy. "How do you suppose we get our paws on it?"

"Well," replied Tyne E., "Milo lets you inside every night while he sleeps. Now, we already know Milo has sold hay to Cheatham in the past. He probably keeps records. All business people do right?"

"I would think so," replied Buddy.

"So then you wait until Milo goes to sleep tonight and look through his records for Cheatham's address," said Tyne E. "It's got to be in the house somewhere."

"You know, come to think of it, there is a brown leather notebook that Milo carries with him. I've seen him tear papers out of it when he sells hay to someone," said Buddy.

"That sounds like a receipt book," said Doc. "It's what I give to all of my customers after I examine them. Well, that and a lolli. The receipt should have the customer's name, and it may have the address. Good thinking, Pickle! If you all need any help, I'll be right here supervising."

"Well then, it's settled, guys," said Tyne E. "Now let's all get some sleep. We're going to need it come tomorrow."

All four friends bedded down for the night. Buddy sneaked through his doggie door to sleep on his usual spot on the sofa. Bird flew back to his nest in the corner of the barn, while Doc caught his z's sitting atop the stall door. Tyne E., all alone and missing his friend P, burrowed under some loose hay in the corner of P's stall. He went to sleep that night imagining how it would feel to sit between P's ears and ride him to victory at the Derby. Tyne E. would finally have his chance to be a real jockey, something he had dreamed of his entire life. But surprisingly, it didn't seem to matter to him as much as it used to. Now, all he wanted, all he could think of, was saving his friend. The reality of the responsibility he was facing began to weigh heavily on his mind. Everyone was counting on him, especially P. As Tyne E. lay there in the hay, seeds of doubt began to enter his thoughts. What if he wasn't a good enough jockey to win the derby? What if he wasn't ready? After all, he had never ridden in a real race. Sure, he and P rode together in Milo's pasture, but running the fence line of a pasture was a far cry from running the rails of a real racetrack. A light chill blew through the barn, and he raised the collar on his coat to cover his neck. He pulled both sides of his coat tightly together and tugged on the cuffs to cover his hands. As he nestled in, he remembered the words that his mom had sewn into his coat when he was just a small mouseling. Tyne E. turned up his cuff, read the words, and said to himself,

"P, I know you can't hear me now, but we're going to win this race. And when we do, you're coming home for good."

Tyne E. smiled, closed his eyes, and drifted off to sleep.

Chapter Eleven

Tyne E. Versus Mr. Weiss

I laid the pages beside the trunk and sat there a moment picking at the splinters of wood peeling from the planks beneath me. I still had another chapter to read, but for the first time since discovering the pages, I thought less about what was happening in the story and more about how it happened. There I was, faced with the challenge of writing something for Mr. Weiss that would completely alter the way he saw just one small mouse. And while sitting there, peeling back thin strips of brittle wood, I imagined my Granddad writing about Tyne E. Did he chew his fingernails like I do? Did he tap his pen against the side of his leg and sit for hours waiting on the right words to come to mind? Or did he know just what to say and how to say it, so that it flowed seamlessly, first onto the page and then into my heart? I didn't know the answer and maybe I never would, but I hoped somehow I could write something that moved Mr. Weiss as much as much as my Granddad's story had moved me. Tyne E. always had faith in his dream, showed unwavering loyalty to his friends, and was willing to face giant hurdles with an attitude of determination that made his three-inch stature seem gargantuan. Tyne E. had grit. And in that quiet moment between chapters, wrestling with the weight of the task before me, I decided, so would I.

I picked up the final chapter and read.

One Last Thing

The next morning Buddy awoke with one thought on his mind: to find that receipt book. He knew he had seen Milo with it before, he just didn't know where Milo kept it. Buddy figured the best way to find the book would be to follow Milo's every step. Eventually, Milo would need the book to look up a customer's number or to mail out a receipt, at least that's what Buddy hoped. So Buddy watched Milo's every move from the moment he got out of bed.

"Yaaaaahhhhh," yawned Milo as he sat up and stretched his arms above his head. "Ohhhh," he mumbled under his breath while he rubbed his forehead.

"Well, you're up early, boy," he said to Buddy. "You must be hungry. Hang on and I'll get you a biscuit." Buddy wagged his tail. If shadowing Milo all day meant extra treat biscuits, Buddy certainly wasn't going to complain. Milo got out of bed and headed to the kitchen to give Buddy his breakfast and make his coffee. The house was still dark with just a small hint of pink light glistening through the windows from the rising sun. Buddy crunched his treat biscuits while Milo stirred the cream and sugar in his coffee and took a loud gulp.

"You know what, boy?" Milo said to Buddy. "Let's you and me go somewhere special today. I think a little time away might do me some good. What do you think, boy?"

Buddy knew the last thing he needed if he was going to find that receipt book was to leave the house, so he did the only thing he knew to do. Buddy rolled over and pretended to be sick. He made the saddest, most pitiful face he could and let out his best puppy-dog whimper.

"What's wrong, Buddy? You don't feel good?" Milo reached down and felt Buddy's nose. "Well, your nose is cold and wet, so you don't have a fever. Is it your tummy? Maybe you ate something bad. You didn't get into the trash can again, did you?" Buddy had a reputation for sneaking into the trash at night while Milo was asleep. It had been the source of a few tummy aches in the past. "I've told you not to do that. There's no telling what you've eaten. We'd better stay here today then. I've got some work to do around the farm anyway. You take it easy today, Buddy," said Milo, and headed toward his room to get dressed.

Buddy spent the whole morning watching Milo work around the house and the farm. Milo did chore after chore, and there was still no sign of the brown leather book. Buddy finally decided that he and his friends may need to orchestrate an intervention, so he headed toward the barn to talk to Tyne E., Doc, and Bird.

"Did you find it?" Tyne E. asked when he saw Buddy.

"No, and I'm beginning to think we may need to do something to speed this up a little. Half the day has gone by, and if we're going to find P tonight, then we need Cheatham's address out of that book. Now, here's what I'm thinking, guys: the only time I've ever seen Milo use the book is when he's doing business with customers. So, I figure the only way we are going to find that book is for someone to order hay."

"Hmmm, good point," replied Tyne E. "But how are we going to get one of Milo's customers to order?"

Buddy smiled, "We aren't. The four of us are going to place the order. Milo goes out to the mailbox to check the mail every evening. I say we write a letter to Milo from Mr. Cheatham asking for more hay. When Milo reads the letter, he'll have to call Cheatham to arrange the pickup of the hay and, bam! We'll have our book!"

"Love it!" said Tyne E. "That should work. Now all we need to do is figure out how we're going to write a letter."

"I've got this," boasted Doc. "Mastering the art of the written word is just one of my many accomplishments in life. Bird, bring me today's newspaper. I'll also need my scalpel and the liquid bandage from my medical kit." Bird flew off to fetch Doc's requests and returned with everything Doc needed to write the letter.

"Now Bird, I'm going to need you to hold a light above my head so that I can make a precise first cut," Doc said to Bird. Bird held the light, and wiped the sweat from Doc's brow as Doc began his project. Doc carefully used his scalpel to cut out each letter he needed to form the words of his note. He then used the liquid bandage to glue the letters to a clean piece of paper Buddy had brought him from inside the house. It took Doc nearly an hour to complete the process, but when he was done, it looked like a sure-enough, bona fide, typewritten masterpiece. Bird flew the letter to the mailbox, placed it inside, and flew back to the barn to wait with his friends.

"Great job, guys," said Buddy. "The bait is set. Now all we have to do is wait." Buddy stayed in the barn with his friends for the next two hours, waiting for Milo to check the mail. Finally, out of the corner of his eye, Buddy saw Milo walking toward the mailbox.

"This is it, guys! He's checking the mail!" Buddy ran out of the barn and headed toward Milo.

"Hey boy!" said Milo to Buddy. "Are you going to help me check the mail today? Well, come on, let's go!" Buddy circled Milo, whining in excitement. "You must be feeling better." Milo pulled a stack of mail out of the mailbox. He sifted through it piece by piece as he walked back to the house. Buddy watched anxiously with every step Milo took. Finally, Milo got to the letter. "Hmmm, this is weird. I didn't think Mr. Cheatham would buy hay from me again after what happened with Pumpernickel and Mayo. Maybe he's had a change of heart! Maybe he'll even let me see Pumpernickel and Mayo. I'd better call him and see how many bales he wants."

Those words were music to Buddy's ears. He knew calling Mr. Cheatham meant finding the receipt book, and finding the receipt book meant learning Mr.

Cheatham's address. Milo and Buddy walked inside. Milo headed toward the kitchen with Buddy on his heels.

"What is it, Buddy?" Milo asked. "You must want a treat biscuit. You can't have any treats now. I have to make a phone call. Later, okay?" Milo picked up the phone and reached for something on the top of the refrigerator.

There it was! The mysterious brown leather receipt book that Buddy had been searching for was on top of the fridge.

No wonder I couldn't find it. I'm way too short to see it up there, Buddy thought.

Milo thumbed through the pages. "Cheatham, Cheatham, Che— Ah, there it is." He dialed the number and waited.

"Yeeehello," answered a deep voice.

"Mr. Cheatham?" asked Milo.

"Yes, who's asking? If you're trying to sell something, I'm not buying," said Cheatham.

"Ugh, no sir, I'm not. Well, I –I am, but it –, it's something you ordered."

"Kid, you've got two seconds to get to the point before I hang up."

"Umm…" said Milo.

"That's one," interrupted Cheatham.

"Sir, I'm not a salesman. This is Milo. I got your letter today about wanting more hay. I was just calling to see how many bales you needed."

"Milo? Kid, I didn't order any hay. If this is some stunt to steal my horse again…"

"No, sir. I have the letter here in my hand."

"That's impossible. Now, I told you before and I'll tell you again: if you want that horse back, you'll have to buy him," snapped Cheatham.

"I understand, but do you think I could at least come see him sometime?" asked Milo.

"Look kid, I have things to do, important things. I'm no babysitter, and this is no animal shelter. If you want to see him, then come to a race. He'll be racing in the Palmetto Derby in less than two weeks. You can see him there from the stands like everyone else."

Click went the phone as Cheatham hung up. Frustrated, Milo tore the page from his receipt book, crumpled it into a tight ball, and threw it into the trashcan.

"I won't be needing this anymore," said Milo. "I'd rather go broke than sell that man one more bale of my hay." Milo stormed out of the kitchen. As soon as he did, Buddy stuck his head into the trashcan and grabbed the crumpled paper. He ran the paper out to the barn.

"I've got it guys, I've got it! Here it is." Buddy dropped the paper in front of Tyne E.

"Why did you crumple it?" asked Tyne E.

"I didn't, Milo did. Never mind that, let's just read it so we can get the address and go visit P," said Buddy.

Tyne E. began to smooth out the wrinkled paper, unfolding each edge until he could make out the words.

"391 Cheatham Road," read Tyne E. aloud. "Wow, Mr. Cheatham even has a road named after him. I should have known. Do you know how to get there, Buddy?"

"I don't. But I'll bet I know someone who does. Hey Bird, do you think you could find 391 Cheatham Road?" asked Buddy.

Bird nodded his head yes.

"Will you take us there tonight?"

Bird raised his wings and flapped them quickly in excitement.

"That means yes," said Doc. "And if Bird is going, then I will be going as well. You never know when you may need the assistance of a doctor. Besides, I'd like to take a look at the zebra before the race. We need to make sure he's in tip-top shape by race day."

That evening, as soon as Milo went to sleep, Buddy sneaked out of the house to meet Tyne E., Bird, and Doc, who were waiting for him in the driveway. The crew of four set off on their journey to Cheatham's farm with Bird leading the way from above.

Bird had a special system for finding his way around areas he'd never been to before. First, he would send out a special chirp alerting all of the other birds in the area to his presence. Then, he would send out a louder chirp letting them know he needed directions. Within minutes, his feathered friends would respond, and a succession of chirps would follow. Now, to the untrained ear, this all sounded like beautiful, carefree music; but to Bird, it was more like calling air traffic control.

Buddy ran along listening to the chirps while keeping his eyes on Bird in the sky. After running to the point of near total exhaustion, Buddy slowed his pace and began to lag behind Bird.

"We're losing them," shouted Doc, who was sitting atop Bird's head as he flew. Bird circled around until he saw Buddy huffing and puffing below. Buddy had gone as far as his paws would take him. He was mustering his last bit of energy to push forward when Bird quickly dived down in front of him and flapped his wings. Bird lifted his right wing and pointed ahead. When Buddy looked up, he saw a sign that read Cheatham Racing Stables.

"Finally," panted Buddy as he huffed and puffed for air. "I couldn't have gone much further. Now we just have to find P."

"He'll be in the stall closest to the turnout pasture," said Tyne E.

"How do you know that?" asked Buddy.

"Because I know my friend. P loves to run. He wouldn't let them cramp him up in a small paddock. I'm telling you, he'll be in a stall that leads to a big turnout pasture. Mark my words, and write that down in whatever you write stuff down in. P will be near a turnout pasture," said Tyne E.

"Okay," replied Buddy. "Then let's start looking. Bird, can you fly up and survey the area?"

Bird surveyed the stables from the air and pointed his wing toward the largest turnout pasture on the entire farm.

"All right, fellas," said Tyne E. to his friends, "let's go find P."

The crew set off in the direction Bird had pointed. Cautious, and aware of the dangers of being in an unfamiliar place, Buddy, Tyne E., Bird, and Doc carefully searched for their friend.

They softly called out P's name until all of a sudden they heard, "Who's that? Who's there?" followed by the loud sound of a horse blowing out air through his lips.

"Relax, it's nothing," said a calm, deep voice. "I'm trying to chill, and you're messing with my vibe. Do you want the rest of that hay?"

Buddy, Tyne E., Bird, and Doc peeked around the corner to see where the voices were coming from, and there was P. He was sharing a stall with another horse: a big, stocky Palomino with a long mane and huge, round hooves.

"P!" said Tyne E. happily. Tyne E. hopped down off Buddy's neck and ran toward his friend.

"Tyne E.!" said P. "Is it really you? You have no idea how glad I am to see you. And Buddy, you came too! Doc, Bird, you're all here! I can't believe it. You all came for me. Quick, break me out of this place so we can go home."

"Well," said Tyne E., looking at the ground. "It's not quite that simple."

"What do you mean? You just open the latch to the stall door. Hop on my head so you can reach it," said P.

"That's not the problem," answered Tyne E. "P, the reason Cheatham came and got you from Milo is because he has papers on you. If we take you back with us, he'll just come and get you again."

"Then what do we do? I can't stay here, guys, I just can't. You don't know what it's like here. The trainers run me everyday, and when I don't run fast enough to suit them, they hit me with their crops. Even when I run as fast as I can, and I feel like my heart is going to explode, they still want me to run faster. I just can't do it anymore, guys! Not to mention, I have no friends and no one to talk to." P hung his head.

"Hey," said the palomino.

"Yes, Hank, you can have my hay," answered P.

"No," said Hank. "That's not what I meant. I was saying hey because I thought *I* was your friend."

"You're right," said P, nodding his head. "You are my friend. And I'm sorry I didn't introduce you. Guys, this is Hank. Hank, this is Buddy, Tyne E., Bird, and that's Doc."

"Nice to meet y'all," replied Hank with his mouth full of hay. "P has told me a lot about y'all, especially you, Tyne E. It sounds like you're a pretty good jockey."

"Thanks. I guess we'll see," answered Tyne E. "That's why we're here. P, we have a plan to get you out of this place, but you'll have to do something I know you're not going to want to do."

"What is it?" asked P timidly.

"You'll have to race in the Palmetto Derby," replied Tyne E. "You'll have to race, and most importantly, you'll have to win."

"But how will winning the derby get me out of here?" asked P. "It will just make old mean Mr. Cheatham want to keep me that much more."

"Not this time!" said Tyne E. "This race will be different. If you win this one, you'll never have to race again if you don't want to. Here's what we're going to do. On the day of the race, Bird will sit atop the main barn at Eastwood Stables and watch for Cheatham's trailer to arrive. Buddy overheard Cheatham tell Milo on the phone that he is going to race you at the derby, so we know he's going to bring you. Bird will let us know which barn Cheatham takes you to, so we can find you. Once you're in your stall, and the coast is clear, my brother Harry is going to give you a full makeover. He'll trim up your mane and dye all your white spots black so that Cheatham won't recognize you. Meanwhile, Bird is going to fly through the window at the racing secretary's office and drop paperwork onto her desk entering *you*, renamed as Peanut Butter and Anything – the last minute, jockeyless mystery stallion – into the race. Of course, you won't actually be jockeyless because I'll be there with you under your racing hood. We'll move you from your stall into one of the empty stalls in the barn until the race begins. When Cheatham's jockey goes to get you for the race, he'll think you've run off again; but Peanut Butter and Anything will be headed to the starting gates for the race."

P interrupted. "But how is me running the race in disguise going to get me out of here and back home with you guys?"

"You didn't let me finish," answered Tyne E. "The paperwork Bird delivers to the racing secretary will list Milo as Peanut Butter and Anything's owner. My brother Tall is taking care of the paperwork to make sure we cross all our T's and dot all our I's. We want everything to be perfect. When you win the race, which I know you will do, the announcer will congratulate Milo as your owner. Milo will get the ten thousand dollar purse, and he will be able to buy you from Mr. Cheatham with the prize money. The plan is foolproof."

"Well that's good, because otherwise I might have to carry out this elaborate plan without the rest of you!" boasted Doc with a smile.

P stood there for a moment without expression as Tyne E., Buddy, and Bird all gave Doc the stink eye.

"So, what do you think?" asked Tyne E.

"What?" replied P. "What do I think about what?"

"The plan," answered Tyne E.

"What plan?" asked P.

"Oh no, I think his amnesia has kicked in again," Tyne E. said as he shook his head. "This happens every time he gets nervous. Hey, P." Tyne E. snapped his fingers in front of P's nose. "Snap out of it, P. Remember the race? We were just talking about the Palmetto Derby and how you have to win it to get out of this place once and for all."

"I'm sorry, I'm sorry," said P. "You know how I am when I get nervous. I just don't know about this race thing, Tyne E. Even talking about it makes me nervous. What's going to happen when I get out on the track? I don't think I can do it. Maybe I'll just run away again."

"No P," said Tyne E. "That's not the answer. You and I both know if you run away, Cheatham will just come and find you and bring you back here. Winning this race is the only way to get your freedom and to come home with all of us."

P looked at them. There sat four of the best friends he had ever known. Tyne E., Buddy, Doc, and Bird would have done anything for him, and he knew it. He had to race, and he had to win. If not for himself, he had to do it for his friends. The four of them had become P's family during his short stay at Milo's farm, and he had to get back to his home.

"You're right. But I can't do it without you as my jockey," P said to Tyne E.

"Don't worry," answered Tyne E. "All I want you to think about until the day of the race is putting one hoof in front of the other as fast as you can. I'll take care of everything else."

With the details settled and P on board with the plan, the crew headed back to Milo's farm. Over the next week and a half, Tyne E. thought of nothing but the race. He spent every waking moment preparing for the big day. He surveyed all of the racing stalls to make sure he knew every detail about the area where P would be on race day. He sneaked into the racing secretary's office and smuggled out a list of all the horses that were entered in the race, and he learned everything there was to know about each of them. At night, he went out to the racetrack and ran the entire track, memorizing every bump and dip in the dirt. During the day, he spent hours reading up on winning jockeys and studying their tactics. Tyne E. left no stone unturned. He was determined to do everything he could to be ready for the big day.

The days passed quickly and before Tyne E. knew it, it was the night before the race. Tyne E. sat alone in his room nervously going over the plan in his mind. He thought out each step and tried to imagine everything going off without a glitch.

"Dinner is ready," yelled Mrs. Tells from down the hall. A few minutes passed, and Tyne E. heard a knock on his bedroom door.

"Come in," said Tyne E.

"Aren't you coming to dinner?" Mrs. Tells asked.

"No, not tonight, Mom. I'm too nervous to eat."

Mrs. Tells smiled lovingly at her son. She knew how much the race meant to him, and how hard he had worked to make sure he was ready.

"Okay, I understand. It's natural to be nervous. But remember, you've worked hard; you've prepared and practiced; and now, you're ready. Tyne E., you've wanted to be a jockey since you were barely old enough to scurry across the floor. Why, I remember the first time you saw the horses run. Your father and I had just moved here to Eastwood. Our first morning here, we went out to the tracks to gather remnants to build our starter burrow. Your brothers were supposed to be watching you back in the barn. Not five minutes had passed since we left the barn, and what do you think I saw out of the corner of my eye?"

"What?" asked Tyne E.

"You! You were barely old enough to get around, yet you had managed to follow your father and me all the way out to the tracks. After that day, you were hooked, and since then, not a day has passed that you haven't dreamed of being a jockey."

Mrs. Tells gently put her hands on her son's shoulders and looked him in the eyes. "What I'm trying to say, Tyne E., is that you're already a winning jockey. Now all you have to do is believe it." Mrs. Tells hugged her son and said goodnight. "I'll leave a plate for you on the counter in case you get hungry," she said as she closed his bedroom door.

That night, after Tyne E.'s family had gone to bed, Tyne E. paced the floor of his bedroom. He knew his mom was right. He knew how important it was to enter the race with confidence, and he wanted P to be able to do the same. But how was he ever going to get P to race without being scared? Tyne E. believed there was an answer to his predicament. After all, he had never faced a problem he couldn't solve. He was a stubborn mouse, and when his mind got set on a goal, nothing could stand in his way. Tyne E. paced his floor for two solid hours until, finally, the answer came to him.

"A coat. That's it! P needs his own coat!" Tyne E. took off his coat and held it out. He ran his fingers across the stitching his mom had sewn. He thought about his scuffle with Robert Newmouse and remembered the courage it took to wrap his coat around Dottie MaeMouse's shoulders all those years ago.

Over time, that coat had become a symbol of Tyne E.'s determination to overcome whatever challenge he faced. It was Tyne E.'s cloak of armor, his lucky charm, and exactly what P needed. Excited, Tyne E. yelled down the hall to wake his mom.

"Mom!" Tyne E. said loudly as he knocked on his parent's bedroom door. "Mom, wake up. I need a favor."

"Tyne E.?" Mrs. Tells said in a groggy voice as she stumbled toward her bedroom door, half asleep. "Tyne E.

it's nearly one o'clock in the morning. Can't this wait? I have a busy day ahead of me tomorrow, and you know how I am if I don't get my beauty sleep."

"I know, and I hate to wake you, but I need your help with something."

"Aaaaahhhhh," yawned Mrs. Tells. "What do you need?"

"I need a tailor-made racing hood," answered Tyne E. "And I need it by morning."

Tyne E. explained how he thought a custom-made racing hood could serve as P's lucky charm the way Tyne E.'s own coat had for him over the years. Eager to help, Mrs. Tells got right to work planning the hood's design. She knew it wouldn't be an easy project, as it was the largest thing she had ever sewn. Mrs. Tells had mastered the art of sewing fine home décor with her custom curtain designs, but a racing hood for a horse was a different matter all together. She would need the whole family's help if she was going to pull this off by morning.

Mrs. Tells went to wake up Tall and Harry while Tyne E. woke his dad.

"Tall," whispered Mrs. Tells as she shook her son's shoulder. "Tall, wake up. I need your help with something."

Tall rolled over and sleepily declared, "If the trap doesn't fit, you must acquit!"

"Tall, wake up," said Mrs. Tells. "You were dreaming about one of your cases again."

"I'm awake, I'm awake," said Tall as he sat up and rubbed his forehead. "I was dreaming about the pj case. My client got caught in a trap by the leg of his pajamas. Luckily, he scurried out of them and got away, but it was a close call. Now he's suing the pj manufacturer."

Mrs. Tells shook her head. "Where's the personal responsibility these days? Anyhow, I need your help with a project for Tyne E. Wake Harry, and meet me in the living room."

The family gathered in the living room, and Mrs. Tells took charge. "Tall and Tyne E., each of you grab an end of the fabric. Harry, I'll need your help cutting." Mrs. Tells looked at her husband. "Honey, you can help me measure." The team got to work. By morning they had made the most beautiful horse hood Tyne E. had ever seen. Mrs. Tells even customized it to match Tyne E.'s coat by designing a one-of-a-kind crest with the letter P placed on the forehead of the hood, which was made of soft, purple silk with white-checkered squares placed evenly throughout. The hood was all Tyne E. had imagined it to be and more, and he couldn't wait to give it to his friend. Having that hood made for P was the last thing Tyne E. needed to do.

Now he was ready.

Chapter Twelve

Aha

I woke up Thursday morning feeling ready as well.
The problem was, I wasn't ready for the right thing. I was
ready to jump out of bed, head down the hall, and climb
the ladder to the attic to see what happened next. I was
ready for P to race. I was ready for Tyne E. to ride P to
victory so Milo could buy him back from Mr. Cheatham
and bring him home. I was ready for more pages, for the
next chapter in Granddad's story. But the problem was,
there were no more pages yet, and I knew I had to wait
all day before I could visit the trunk again to find out

what happened. It was pure torture, but I had to go to school and wait for the revelation of P's fate.

I got up and shuffled across the white shag rug beside my bed. I opened my closet doors to pick out an outfit, but something blocked one of the doors halfway. My backpack, the stack of paper I had left completely blank, and a pen lay there, silently reminding me that I wasn't ready for Mr. Weiss' assignment. I had one day, one day to write my paper and thwart an unwanted fate for my one mouse.

As soon as I got to school, I told Kristen about my meeting with Mr. Weiss and about the paper. The entire day, all I could think of was that paper. I didn't have a topic, I didn't have a title, and I didn't even have an idea. By the fifth period bell, my mind was in total disarray.

"So, any ideas yet?" Kristen asked.

"Um, what? Oh yeah, um, no not yet." I sputtered like an old truck with a worn-out engine.

"It'll come to you. That's how the best ideas happen. They pop in your head out of nowhere, and bam, problem solved!" Kristen was always the optimist. She was right though. I knew something would come to me. I just wasn't sure what that something would be, or if it was going to come to me in time.

"Okay, class. Everybody get quiet and take your seats," instructed Mr. Weiss. "Today is our mouse dissection question and answer session. Now, to recap the week – classes were cancelled Tuesday because of the unfortunate *bacon burning bonanza*, at least that's what I've heard you guys are calling it." Mr. Weiss chuckled as if he'd been invited to join an inside joke. "Because of that, we had to condense our mouse anatomy study and our dissection video viewing into one day. Now is your opportunity to ask questions about the material we went over yesterday, so you will be prepared for tomorrow's dissection. Remember, this project will be heavily weighted for your final grade, so don't take this lightly."

Billy was the first to raise his hand.

"Yes, Billy," said Mr. Weiss, pointing his finger in Billy's direction.

"So the mice won't be light?"

"Light?" questioned Mr. Weiss.

"Yes," replied Billy, "because of them being weighted."

Mr. Weiss squinted at Billy. Trying to comprehend the weird way Billy's brain worked, he answered, "No, the mouse will not be weighted. Your grade for the dissection will be weighted. In other words, Billy, you need to do well on this project." Mr. Weiss shook his head. "Any more questions?" No one raised a hand. "Come on guys, this is your last chance before you pick up the scalpel. Someone must have a question." No one said a word. "All right then, I'll just give you the rest of the period to have quiet study if nobody has any…" Mr. Weiss suddenly spotted a hand rising amid the sea of bored and disinterested students. "Yes, Ms. Emerson."

Oh no, it's Kristen. What's she going to say? I thought. *Please don't say anything about the paper.*

"Mr. Weiss, I think the class should be aware of the grave injustice that is about to take place in this very room tomorrow and the fact that my friend here is going to do her part to sway the tide of tragedy and save a life."

"Ms. Emerson, I've already discussed the matter with Ms. Ashford."

"Wait, what?" asked one of the cheerleaders sitting in the back of the classroom.

"Yeah, that's right," declared Kristen. "Savannah has accepted Mr. Weiss' challenge to write a paper defending the importance of one little mouse, and if it's a good paper, then Mr. Weiss has agreed to spare her mouse." The class began to stir and chatter. Mr. Weiss quickly sensed a rebellion brewing and attempted to quiet the heckling cheerleader squad in the back row.

"That's enough. Raise your hands. Raise your hand if you want to speak. One at a time," he said.

His reflexes being sharper than his brain, Billy was the first to raise his hand.

"Yes, Billy?" asked Mr. Weiss.

"Since the mouse is supposed to be weighted, and Savannah is writing a paper, can I just make a paperweight in exchange for not dissecting a mouse?"

"No Billy, you still have to dissect a mouse to pass the class," said Mr. Weiss.

"Hey, that's not fair. Equal opportunity!" said Kristen.

"Yeah! Equal opportunity!" agreed the cheerleading squad in the back row. Before I knew it, the class had erupted in full revolt.

"Protect, don't dissect! Protect, don't dissect! Protect, don't dissect!" they chanted. Mr. Weiss tried to temper the uproar with hand motions and shushing. I could have told him that wasn't going to work and saved his deltoids the effort, but he shushed with both arms in the air for nearly two whole minutes before finally writing these words on the chalkboard – IF ONE MOUSE, THEN ALL MICE. Thinking back on it, it was an ingenious phrase to write. Those words said just enough to make the class stop chanting and ask, *what*?

When the noise lessened, Mr. Weiss smiled. Before anyone had a chance to ask, he explained, "I can see this is an important topic for more of you than just Savannah."

"Ahem!" Kristen cleared her throat.

"And Ms. Emerson," Mr. Weiss nodded in reply. "So I'll make this deal for all of you. If Ms. Ashford submits a paper worthy of saving her one mouse, then I will allow all of you to skip the dissection."

What? I panicked. My mind began racing with thoughts of the entire class chanting at me rather than Mr. Weiss as they had just moments before his chalky proposal.

"Ms. Ashford," said Mr. Weiss. The whole class turned to look at me. I could feel my face getting hotter with each passing second. I tried to force my mouth into a semi-smile, but it wouldn't stick. My beet-red cheeks trembled with trepidation.

"It's up to you to spare the class's mice." The class fell silent. Mr. Weiss fell silent. The only sound was that of my throat choking down the huge gulp of air that I'd just swallowed.

Say something, Savannah, I thought, as if it would help to put even more pressure on myself than Mr. Weiss just had. I remembered Tyne E., and I thought about race day. I suddenly realized this was it. This was the lead-up to my race day. Then, I did something no one expected, not even myself. I stood up from my desk and walked to the chalkboard. My eyes remained fixated on one word. When I reached the front of the room, I took the chalk right out of Mr. Weiss' hand. The sound that small piece of chalk made when it hit the chalkboard must have been heard all around the school because when I used it to slash through the word *IF*, I became an instant celebrity at Ward Middle.

By the end of the day, everyone knew about the dissection revolt, and my dear friend Kristen had proclaimed me as the leader of the movement by passing around handwritten flyers after school. *Thanks alot, Kristen.* The pressure was intense, the expectations were heavy, but the challenge had been given to me. And I had accepted it. I knew it wouldn't be easy, and I still wasn't sure what I would write about. But I believed I would win. And the funny thing was, just like Tyne E.'s mom had told him, when I started believing it, everyone else did as well.

Inspired by the events of the day, I went home that night with a plan. I would read the rest of Granddad's story, and use it as motivation to write my paper. When I got home from school, I barreled through the door and headed straight for the attic. I opened the trunk expecting to see the next chapter, but what I saw instead was the empty, splintery bottom of the old wooden trunk. I wasn't sure what to think. The trunk had always functioned like clockwork. Every day since I'd discovered the trunk I'd found new pages, so why not now? Why not when I needed them most? I closed the lid, waited a moment, and opened it again – nothing. There was not one page for me to read, not even one paragraph.

Not knowing what to do, I closed the lid and went back to my room to search through the thick stack of pages I had found in the trunk over the past week. *Maybe I missed something*, I thought. I began digging through the chapters. I shuffled them, urgently looking for the note my granddad had written me.

"Aha, there you are!" When I found the note, I read it again.

> *My Sweet Savvy,*
>
> *My messenger is small, so my words must be few. He'll bring them each night, but only to you.*
>
> *You are my heart,*
> *Granddad*

"Okay," I said aloud. "It says each *night*. So I'll wait. Maybe it's too early." But, in my heart, I knew the time didn't have anything to do with the trunk being empty. After all, I had visited the trunk at that time of day before and still found pages. I was searching for any explanation. I didn't want to accept the possibility that the pages had stopped before I found out what happened to Tyne E. and P.

I spent the rest of the afternoon sitting against the headboard of my bed with a stack of blank papers propped atop my crisscrossed legs. If staring at white paper could have turned blank lines into prose, then I would have completed my project within the first hour. I checked the time on the clock by my bed, 5:20 p.m. I knew we wouldn't have dinner for another hour, so I leaned my head back and closed my eyes. I must have been exhausted from the excitement of the day, because I don't even remember falling asleep. The next thing I knew, I was waking up to a dark room. I checked my clock and it said 9:13 p.m.

"Oh no! I fell asleep!" I jumped up with the stack of blank papers clutched tightly in my hand, stumbled across my room, and flipped on the light switch. "This is bad. This is so bad. I'm going to have to stay up all night to finish this paper now." I threw the papers onto the floor, and when I did, they landed right beside Granddad's note. I remembered the trunk. Wasting not one second, I opened the door and rushed down the hall. When I passed the kitchen, I saw my mom had left me a plate of food on the table with a yellow sticky note that read,

Found you sleeping this afternoon and figured you needed the rest. There's a piece of your favorite pie in the refrigerator! XOXO!!   *Mom*

As nice as that pie would have been, I didn't have time to eat. Like a beacon that kept luring me toward it, I couldn't resist the pull of the trunk. I pulled the ladder from the attic and climbed the steps. I steadily paced toward the trunk and reached for the lid. My hand trembled just enough to telegraph my current state of anticipation. I steadied my fingers by shaking them and wiping my palms against my thighs. I reached for the trunk and lifted the lid.

"Pictures!" I said aloud. There had never been pictures before, only papers. At first I wasn't sure whether to pick up the pictures or close the lid. I'm not going to lie – it kind of scared me. The peculiar idea of pages spontaneously appearing in the attic had finally become normal to me, and now there were pictures. I took a deep breath, steadied my hands for the second time, and reached into the trunk. I pulled out the stack of pictures and heard TAT TATTATtattattattat ta tatatisss.

Startled, I dropped the pictures all over the floor. I quickly tiptoed over to the ladder to listen for my mom. I stood there a second and heard the sound again. TAT TATTATtattattattat ta tatatisssss.

I looked around wondering what unimaginable monster could have made that sound, then realized it was just our old air conditioner. It had been threatening to go out on us for the past two summers. "Phew!" After slowing my racing heart, I turned to walk back to the trunk and saw the pictures scattered on the floor. I couldn't believe what I was seeing. There was Granddad, young, happy, and full of life. He was standing in front of a green and white barn that had stacks of hay all around it. On the right side of Granddad sat the happiest looking dog I'd ever seen, with one crooked ear and almond-shaped eyes. On the other side, attached to a lead line, stood a tall, lanky, black and white Paint horse.

Was it real? I thought. I knew it couldn't actually be a true story. After all, animals can't talk, and mice don't ride horses. "No, it's impossible," I whispered under my breath. I gathered up all of the pictures and placed them back in the trunk exactly as I had found them. I closed the trunk and began to tiptoe toward the ladder. As I did, I saw something small run across the floor in front of me. I quickly pulled out my flashlight and shined it around the floor like a searchlight. I heard something behind me, spun around, and spotted two small eyes staring back at me. It was a mouse! We both stood there for a moment, frozen, each waiting for the other to make a move. What happened next I've carried with me to this very day. The mouse, who I remember looking like a perfectly normal house mouse, walked across the floor, upright like a little human: one with big ears and a long tail. He strolled toward Granddad's trunk, as if he hadn't a care in the world, climbed up the side, lifted the lid, and disappeared.

I rubbed my eyes and refocused them. I shined my light all around the floor beneath the trunk. I made my way over to the trunk, stepping gingerly, putting weight on my toes first so as not to make a sound. I was scared, but I knew I had to open it. My curiosity wouldn't let me pretend I had not seen what I knew I had. I slowly opened the trunk, fully expecting to see a small mouse inside. What I saw instead was a stack of blank papers, a pen, and a note.

Savannah,

More than anything, I want to finish this story for you. I try to find the words, but they keep slipping away. What I've written is a part of me. It's who I was and who I am.

Milo is the young man I once was before this illness began to steal my memories. Buddy is the voice of reason that keeps me focused through each confusing new day. Doc is my treatment, a reminder that even though the doctors say they know what they are doing, I often have my doubts. Bird is my hope and the loyalty that people I love dearly have shown to me. P is my mind, my thoughts, and my memories. Cheatham is the illness that is trying to steal them from me.

Tyne E., I've saved for last because he is the most important. Tyne E. Tells is the love. He's the love

I have for you and the courage I use to face the challenge of each new day. Savvy, love is stronger than any Cheatham either of us will ever face, and love is why you are reading this note. Love is my messenger, and this is my message to you…

My sweet Savvy, you are the rest of my story.

Through tear-filled eyes I looked down into the depths of that old trunk one last time that very special night. Under the blank papers lay a small coat no bigger than my hand. "Could it be?" I murmured. I picked up the coat, turned up the sleeve, and read,

Write your story.

Every day is meaningful and special in its own way, but very few days are purely unforgettable – this had been one of those few days. I knew in that moment that Tyne's destiny was mine to create. My granddad had written for me, and now it was my turn to write for him.

Chapter Thirteen

I Wrote All Night

Without thinking, without questioning, I picked up the blank papers and began to fill them using the pen my granddad had left for me…

By a Hair, By a Nose, By a Pickle

As soon as the sun rose, Tyne E. and his brothers headed to the track to await P's arrival. When they got there, they saw Bird and Doc perched on top of the barn where all the horses that would be racing that day were kept.

"Bird!" Tyne E. called out, waving his hands in the air. "Down here!"

Bird saw Tyne E. and flew down to meet him.

"Have you seen Cheatham's trailer pull in yet?" Tyne E. asked.

"The old grump pulled in about five minutes ago," replied Doc. "P is already unloaded and in his stall. He looked nervous. But I guess that's to be expected for a zebra who's about to run in a horse race. Who are your friends, Tyne E.?" asked Doc.

"Oh, I'm sorry. I should have introduced you all. Doc, Bird, these are my brothers, Tall and Harry. Tall, Harry, this is Doc and Bird."

Doc gave a hello salute with one of his many feet. "Nice to meet you both. FYI, I am a doctor, so if either of you is in need of medical services, please see my assistant Bird who can schedule you for a checkup. I am the best in my field. You've probably already heard of me – most have. I'm the zebra's doctor. I'm here to make sure he is in tip-top shape for this race."

Not wanting to be outdone by Doc, Tall replied, "I'm a lawyer. I've prepared the paperwork for P, also known as Peanut Butter and Anything, to race in this derby. I've ensured that said horse will be racing under Milo's ownership so he can win the ten thousand dollar purse and buy said horse's freedom. Without me, the plan would be futile."

"Well, I suppose someone has to do the easy part," Doc said with a smile stretched across his hairy cheeks.

"All right, guys," interrupted Tyne E, "let's get this show on the road. Tall – you, Bird, and Doc deliver the paperwork through the window of the racing secretary's office just like we planned. Harry – you come with me, and we'll find P."

So Bird, with Doc hitching a ride atop his head and Tall hanging on to his foot, flew toward the racing secretary's office.

"Nice and easy now, Bird. Heights aren't really my thing," said Tall through his chattering teeth.

"Onward and upward, Bird!" shouted Doc, with one of his fingers pointed in the air. "Tall!" Doc yelled loudly so Tall could hear him over the wind. "Look down! I hear it helps."

Bird flew over the barns and across the track toward the entrance to the stables. As he neared the racing secretary's office, he could see the open window. Bird chirped and pointed his wing to let Doc and Tall know that he was going in for the dive. Bird lowered his head, aimed the tips of his wings directly behind him and flew straight toward the window. Just as he was about to make his heroic entrance it happened. THUMP! Bird's beak hit glass.

"Oh my stars! Heavens to Betsy!" screamed the head secretary from inside the office. "That bird was trying to attack me! Did you see?" she asked the other secretary who worked there. "He was headed straight for the window!"

"Bless your heart," said the other secretary. "Are you okay? There's no tellin' what that bird would have done if he had gotten in here. Thank goodness you shut the window when you did. Why, if the boss man would let us run the air conditioner a little more, we wouldn't have to keep it open all the time. But you know he's so tight he could squeeze a quarter and make the eagle scream. I'm gonna go to the break room and make us both some iced tea. We're gonna need it with that window closed. It'll be hotter in here than a billy goat's rear in a pepper patch by the end of the day."

Bird hovered at the window listening.

"Well, this is just great," said Tall. "How are we going to get the paperwork in there now? By the way, Bird, this may be a bad time to bring this up, but we could have a case of slander against these ladies, not to mention defamation of character and damages from personal injury. How's your neck?"

Bird chirped and cocked his head to the side.

"Here, take my card," said Tall.

Doc interrupted, "No worries. You forget there is a doctor in the house. Bird, do you feel okay to fly?"

Bird shook his head.

Doc leaned forward to take a look at his patient. "I think you have a bruised beak. When we get home, we'll soak it in ice cream. You'll be fine." Doc patted Bird on the head. "Now, what was Plan B?"

"Plan B?" replied Tall. "Why are you asking me?"

"You mean to say you don't have a Plan B?" asked Doc.

"Now hold on a second. I was only supposed to prepare the paperwork, which I did to exact perfection using my advanced intellect and superior talents," said Tall. "You and Bird were supposed to get the paperwork into the office. I did my part."

While Tall and Doc argued about who was to blame for their situation, Bird spotted a crack in the foundation of the building. He quickly dove down and hovered in front of the crack to show it to Doc and Tall.

"Easy with the sudden movements, Bird. I'm hanging on for dear life here," said Tall as he gripped Bird's leg tightly.

"Aha!" said Doc proudly. "Look there. Right there is a crack. It's a good thing I'm here. You two would be lost without me."

Bird landed on the ground, and Tall walked toward the crack. While Tall peeked inside the foundation crack, Doc came up with Plan B.

"Listen up, you two," said Doc. "Here's what we're going to do. Tall, you enter the building through this crack, and make your way up to the office. Bird and I will hold onto the paperwork, since it won't fit through the crack. Once you're in the office, climb up to the windowsill and cause a distraction. Do whatever you have to do to get those two ladies to open that window. When they open the window, Bird will fly in with the paperwork, drop it on the desk, and fly out."

Tall put his paw to his forehead and sighed. "How did I get myself into this?" he whispered under his breath.

"What's that?" asked Doc.

"I said it sounds like a plan," replied Tall reluctantly as he walked toward the building. "So long, fellas. I'll see you both on the other side of the window."

While Tall, Doc, and Bird handled one crisis, Tyne E. and Harry had encountered another.

"This dye isn't taking, Tyne E.," said Harry as he put the third application of hair dye onto P's white spots. "I don't know what to do! We're almost out of dye, and these white patches are turning brown instead of black. He looks awful! He can't race like this."

"Hang on, I have an idea," said Tyne E. "I'll be right back."

"Wait, where are you going?" yelled Harry as Tyne E. scurried off.

"Trust me!" Tyne E. yelled over his shoulder. Tyne E. ran as fast as he could back toward his home. His dad had just finished a big construction job the week before, and Tyne E. remembered seeing leftover paint supplies in his dad's tool shed burrow. When he reached home, he quickly rummaged through the shed, climbing stacks of old wood and throwing tools over his shoulder as he searched. *They've got to be here.* Then he saw them. Covered in sawdust, in the corner of the shed, was a stack of cans – black paint cans.

"Yes!" Tyne E. loaded a wheelbarrow with buckets of the paint. *This should do the trick.* He scurried back to the stables as quickly as he could, trying not to spill the buckets.

"Here you go," said Tyne E. excitedly, as he ran through the stall door with the wheelbarrow. "You can use this to finish dying P's spots."

"Paint!" exclaimed Harry. "You expect me to do my best work with paint? That's like asking Mozart to play his music with a kazoo! I cannot, I will not use paint on a client's hair."

With both paws, Tyne E. grabbed Harry's face and squished his cheeks together. "Harry, we're running out of time. Now, stop being dramatic. Use the paint!"

Harry sighed. "Well, is it latex or oil based?"

"It's latex."

"Fine, then. At least it will wash off easily. Pass me a brush. Let's do this," said Harry in a determined voice. "We're going to give a whole new meaning to the term Paint horse."

When Harry was done, P looked spectacular. Not one white hair was left on his body. He was covered from head to hoof in solid jet-black color.

"How do I look?" asked P.

"Like you've just been to see the best stylist of all time!" boasted Harry.

"You look great, P," answered Tyne E. "There's just one problem."

"Oh no, what?" asked P in a panic. "There can't be any problems!"

"P, it's just a figure of speech," said Tyne E. "Stay calm. You don't want your amnesia to kick in before the race even starts."

"You're right, you're right," replied P. "Breathe in, breathe out, breathe in, breathe out."

"Here," said Tyne E. "You can't race without a racing hood. I had it made especially for you. When you put this hood on, I want you to believe that we've already won this race. This racing hood will soon be known as the hood worn by the winning horse in the Palmetto Derby!"

P lowered his head while Tyne E. and Harry put the hood on him.

"Now just remember," Tyne E. said to P, "I'll be sitting right between your ears. All you have to do is put one hoof in front of the other as fast as you can. I'll take care of the rest."

"Got it," said P.

"RIDERS, MAKE YOUR WAY TO THE GATES," announced a loud, deep voice over the intercom.

"It's time," said Tyne E. "Quick, P, we have to get you out of here before Cheatham's jockey comes looking for you." Tyne E. jumped on P's head.

"Wait, guys," said Harry. "Where are Tall, Doc, and Bird? Shouldn't they have been back already?"

"You're right. They've been gone far too long," replied Tyne E.

"What are we going to do?" asked P.

"We can't wait here, that's for sure. We have to head toward the gates," said Tyne E.

"But what if they didn't get the paperwork delivered to the secretary's office?" asked P in a panic.

Tyne E. patted P's head to keep him calm. "We can't worry about that now. We'll just have to trust that they did."

P and Tyne E. began their long walk toward the starting gates just as Tall finished his long climb to the second floor of the racing secretary's office.

Huffing and puffing, Tall complained to himself the whole way. "I can't believe I got stuck with this job. And all for a piece of crumb cake! That darn crumb cake is so addictive. Just say no, Tall. Just say no." Tall scurried through the wall until he found an opening into the office. The two secretaries sat sorting through the last minute race entries. He looked his two opponents over, carefully assessing the best plan of action. Every mouse who has ever been a mouse decoy knows success is in the planning, but time was creeping up on him.

"I think these are the last of the entries," Tall heard one of the secretaries say.

"They'd better be. The cutoff is in five minutes," replied the other secretary. "Hand them here, and I'll log them."

Tall knew he had to act right away if Bird was going to have time to fly P's paperwork through the window before the cutoff.

"Here goes," said Tall. He took off running across the room, squeaking as loudly as he could to draw the attention of the secretaries.

"Aaaaaaaa!" screeched the head secretary. "Heavens to Betsy, it's a mouse! Get the broom!"

Tall scurried toward the window, ran up the curtain, and jumped onto the windowsill.

"Where did it go?" the assistant secretary yelled as she jumped onto the seat of her chair. "There it is! It's on the windowsill. Shoo him out!"

The head secretary waved her hands at Tall, but Tall just ran back and forth, dodging her clumsy moves.

"Open the window!" yelled the head secretary's assistant. As soon as the head secretary opened the window, Bird flew from around the corner and nosedived into the office carrying P's paperwork in his beak. SMACK! Bird flew square into the head secretary, and she fell back onto her chair. The chair rolled across the floor into the assistant secretary who was still standing on her chair trying to avoid the mouse. While the two secretaries toppled over one another, Bird flapped his wings over the desk, and all the papers went flying into the air. Bird dropped P's race registration papers onto the jumbled pile and flew out of the window, picking up Tall with only seconds to spare, before the head secretary came after him swinging a broom.

"Call for backup! Call an exterminator! Call the zoo!" she shouted.

"What do I tell them?" asked the assistant secretary as she tried to pick up the phone, fumbling it in her panic.

"Tell them there's a rogue attack bird and a rabid mouse on the loose here at Eastwood! Hurry!"

A few minutes later, as Tyne E. and P headed toward the starting gate, they heard an announcement come over the loud speaker.

"ATTENTION ALL PATRONS! ATTENTION ALL PATRONS! PLEASE BE ON THE LOOKOUT FOR A LONE BARN SWALLOW WHO MAY BE PRONE TO ATTACK. HE WAS LAST SPOTTED AT THE MAIN OFFICE WITH A POSSIBLE MOUSE ACCOMPLICE. IF YOU SEE THE ATTACK BIRD, REMAIN CALM AND REPORT THE SIGHTING TO THE NEAREST EASTWOOD STABLE EMPLOYEE. THANK YOU FOR YOUR COOPERATION, AND ENJOY THE RACE."

"That's Bird and Tall!" said Tyne E.

"So this means they got the paperwork delivered in time?" asked P.

"I hope so. We won't know for sure until they announce your name as Peanut Butter and Anything.

And there's only one way to get the announcer to call out your name – head toward the gate," Tyne E. said.

As Tyne E. and P approached the starting gate, the crowd of spectators began to thicken. Among them was none other than old man Cheatham who was grouchy as ever, especially after having been told that his prized racehorse, Pumpernickel and Mayo, had once again run off and was presently nowhere to be found. As Mr. Cheatham's jockey and trainer broke the news of P's untimely escape to him, Milo, with Buddy by his side, made his way up and along the stadium seating to find just the right spot to see his old pal P race in the Palmetto Derby.

"I sure hope he wins," Milo said to Buddy, carefully sitting down while juggling his soda, a small box of popcorn, and a country ham biscuit – a must-have for every hungry spectator at the Derby.

"Here ya go, boy," said Milo as he tore a piece of ham from his biscuit and offered it to Buddy. Buddy took the ham between his front teeth and let it fall to the ground.

"You don't like it?" asked Milo. Buddy just looked ahead at the track, completely ignoring Milo. He was too nervous to eat. "All right, then I'll eat it all by myself," Milo said with a mouthful of ham biscuit.

Br-br-bru-bru-bru-bru-bru-bru-bru-bru-bru-bru-bru-br-bruuuum! The bugle rang out as the horses approached the gate.

"THIS IS A GREAT LINE UP TODAY, FOLKS! IT OUGHT TO BE A GOOD RACE!" called out the announcer. "THE HORSES ARE LOADING INTO THE GATE."

One by one the announcer said the names of the horses as they loaded into the gate.

"AND IN GATE FIVE, WE HAVE A NEWCOMER TO THE RACE, THE JOCKEYLESS, JET-BLACK STALLION – PEANUT BUTTER AND ANYTHING. THIS IS PEANUT BUTTER AND

ANYTHING'S FIRST TIME RACING IN THE
PALMETTO DERBY, AND A FIRST ENTRY FOR HIS
OWNER – MILO."

Milo nearly choked on his popcorn when he heard
the announcer say his name.

"So you entered the race, huh, kid?" yelled a deep
voice from high in the stands. Milo looked up to see Mr.
Cheatham with his hands cupped around both sides of
his mouth. "I'll tell ya what," yelled Cheatham. "You win
this purse, and it will be just enough to buy the horse you
tried to steal from me." Cheatham knew P was missing,
but the old man was just mean and sneaky enough to try
to sell Milo a missing horse. "Come see me if you win,
kid. I'll sign P's papers over to you, and you can pick him
up on the way out."

"But I didn't enter a horse into the…" Milo wasn't
able to finish his sentence before he heard the words,

"AND THEY'RE OFF!"

P shot from the gate as if he was born to do nothing other than run that one race. His hooves drove over the dirt like a high-speed freight train. Before any of the other horses had even cleared the gates, P had already taken the lead by three full strides. Tyne E. clenched P's mane between his fingers as tightly as he could. The pounding of hooves beneath him made his small hands vibrate so much that he could barely keep his grip, but Tyne E. didn't even care. This was the moment he had waited for his entire life. He was finally a jockey in a real horse race.

"You're winning, P! You're winning!" shouted Tyne E. in P's ear. "The closest horse is at least ten lengths back."

P, barreling forward with blinders on either side of his eyes, shouted back at Tyne E., "I'm winning? Should I slow down? Maybe I should save some energy for the last half. I could be pacing myself better."

"P!" shouted Tyne E., "Just run – run like you're still in the pastures at Milo's farm. Run like you've just heard the dinner bell. Run!"

P picked up his stride. By the time Tyne E. finished the last words of his pep talk and took a deep breath, P led the race by nearly half the track. No horse had ever gained that much of a lead in the history of the Derby. The race was all but won, until Tyne E. felt something hit his nose. It was the one thing he hadn't planned on – rain. The drops began to fall one after another. Faster and faster they fell as P ran under the rain cloud that had formed over the track.

Oh no! Tyne E. thought. *This could ruin everything. The paint could wash off before we make it to the finish line!* Suddenly, the rain began to fall as if buckets of water were being poured from the sky. P's hooves started to slip in the mud, and water dripped into his eyes.

"I can't see, Tyne E.!" P yelled. "I can't…whoa whooooaaah!" THUMP, went P's body as it hit the mud, shaking the ground beneath him. Tyne E. tried his best to hang on, but the force of the fall was just too much. He was thrown forward into the thick muck. The other horses were quickly approaching. Tyne E. had to get back on P as fast as he could.

"P!" Tyne E. called out. "P, are you okay? Can you get up?" P stood up and shook. Mud went everywhere, camouflaging Tyne E. even worse than he already was.

"Tyne E.!" P called out. "Where are you? I don't see you!"

"I'm here!" yelled Tyne E. "Hurry, I'm stuck! The mud is too thick!"

P began to panic. He saw the other horses gaining ground, and he knew he only had moments to find Tyne E. before they trampled his friend. Suddenly, P froze in fear. He couldn't move a muscle, and he couldn't answer Tyne E.

Oh no! thought Tyne E. *His amnesia has kicked in.* Tyne E. yelled as loudly as he could. "P! P! P! Snap out of it, P!" *This is it*, thought Tyne E. *I'm done for. This is the end*. With the horses almost upon him, Tyne E. squeezed his eyes together tightly and prepared for the worst. But just as he braced himself for impact, he felt something grab his coat collar and lift him into the air.

"LADIES AND GENTLEMEN, THE ATTACK BIRD AND HIS MOUSE ACCOMPLICE HAVE BEEN SPOTTED ON THE TRACK. PLEASE STAY CALM AND REMAIN IN YOUR SEATS," said the announcer over the loud speaker.

Bird, Doc, and Tall had swooped in just in time to rescue Tyne E. from the fast-approaching field of horses. Bird tossed Tyne E. into the air so that he would land squarely between P's ears.

Everything began to make sense to Milo. The bird on the track was no attack bird, the mouse was no ordinary mouse, and the mysterious jockeyless racehorse was not without a jockey. The mouse he had seen riding P in his pasture months before was now racing in the

Palmetto Derby, which meant the horse he was riding had to be none other than P! Milo couldn't fathom who would have orchestrated such a plan, but he knew if the mysterious jockeyless racehorse won the Derby, he would get the ten thousand dollar purse he needed to buy P from Mr. Cheatham.

Milo jumped from his seat and raised his hands in the air. "Go, Peanut Butter and Anything, go!" Buddy barked with excitement. Side by side, the two cheered on Tyne E. and P as if the outcome of the race depended upon it.

After landing perfectly between P's ears, Tyne E. grabbed P's mane and leaned forward. With only seconds to spare, Tyne E. spoke the magic words that P needed to hear, and P bolted from a dead stop to a full run in half a second. The rest of the horses were neck-and-neck with P. Tyne E. pulled P's mane left and right to steer him through the field of competitors. The ground shook as all of the horses fiercely rounded the corner to the finish line.

"This is it, P: the final push," said Tyne E. "Give it all you've got." Tyne E. was holding on to P's mane so tightly that his small hands were shaking. It was all he could do to keep his grip. He knew if P picked up speed, he may not be able hold on, but he had no other choice. Saving his friend was all that mattered to Tyne E.

"Run, P, run!" Tyne E. yelled. And P did just that. Tyne E. began to lose his grip, but P was gaining ground.

"Are you okay, Tyne E.?" yelled P.

"Run!" answered Tyne E.

P began to emerge from the group.

"AND IT'S PEANUT BUTTER AND ANYTHING TAKING THE LEAD. PEANUT BUTTER AND ANYTHING IS OUT IN FRONT. PEANUT BUTTER AND ANYTHING…" said the announcer.

Just as P took the lead, Tyne E. lost his grip. He toppled backward from between P's ears and down the back of P's neck. When Tyne E. reached the base of P's neck, a button on his coat snagged the bottom of P's racing hood. Tyne E. grabbed the fabric and pulled himself up onto P's neck. He could see the finish line ahead.

"PEANUT BUTTER AND ANYTHING HAS THE LEAD! IT'S PEANUT BUTTER AND ANYTHING BY TWO LENGTHS, NOW THREE, NOW FOUR… AND PEANUT BUTTER AND ANYTHING WINS THE PALMETTO DERBY!" yelled the announcer. "CONGRATULATIONS TO OUR NEWEST WINNER OF THE PALMETTO DERBY, PEANUT BUTTER AND ANYTHING, AND TO HIS OWNER, MILO!"

Milo leapt with pride before running down the steps of the spectator stands and heading toward the office to claim the winner's purse. He was so eager to get the prize money that he nearly tripped over Buddy.

"Come on, Buddy. We're going to buy P from Mr. Cheatham and bring him home. Finally!"

Milo claimed the winner's purse and took the money straight to Mr. Cheatham, who was still in the stands.

"Here you are, sir," said Milo proudly as he handed Mr. Cheatham the full payment of ten thousand dollars. "I believe you told me the price to buy P back from you was ten thousand dollars. Well, there it is. Count it if you want."

Mr. Cheatham smirked. "No kid, that won't be necessary. In fact, I think I'll go ahead and sign over his registration papers to you right now. You can pick him up in the holding stalls behind the track." Mr. Cheatham leaned down, opened his briefcase, and handed the papers to Milo along with a bill of sale. Milo took the papers and began to walk away.

"Good luck finding him, kid," old mean Mr. Cheatham said smugly, thinking he had just tricked Milo.

Milo never turned around. He just smiled, looked toward the track ahead and said, "Oh, I don't think I'll have a problem."

When Milo reached the Winner's Circle, he saw P – or shall we say, Peanut Butter and Anything – standing proudly with flowers draped over his neck. Photographers were snapping pictures left and right, trying to get the perfect shot of the newest Palmetto Derby winner. But as much as Milo wanted to let P stay and bask in the glory of victory, he spotted a gleam of pearly white hair near the bottom of P's right back leg just above his hoof. Some of the paint had begun to wear off, and Milo knew he needed to get P out of there right away before anyone else noticed. Milo stepped forward through the crowd and took P by the fabric of his racing hood.

"That will be all for now, folks. I need to get him home to rest up," said Milo as he led P through the crowd toward the stables. When they got a good distance from everyone, Milo stopped and said, "All right P, where's your friend?"

P didn't budge. He acted as if Milo hadn't said a word.

"I know he's under there. I've seen the two of you together in the pasture, and I saw him today during the race. It's okay, P, any friend of yours is a friend of mine. Not to mention that I'd like to have the honor of meeting the winning jockey in this year's Palmetto Derby."

Right then, Tyne E. popped his head out from under the hood. "So you're the mouse jockey I saw in my pasture that morning." Milo smiled. "Well it's nice to meet you." Milo extended his hand to Tyne E. "How about we switch places? P, can you give me a ride home? And you, little guy," Milo said to Tyne E., "you can ride right here in my pocket."

Tyne E. scurried from P's neck up Milo's arm and into his pocket. With Buddy faithfully by their sides, Milo jumped on P's back, and the four of them headed home. Tyne E. settled comfortably in Milo's pocket while sporting the biggest grin ever seen on a mouse. A slight breeze lifted the sleeve of Tyne E.'s coat, and he caught a glimpse of the golden thread his mom had used to sew that special message so long ago.

Then, Tyne E. Tells – the mouse who knew what he wanted and dared to go get it – turned his sleeve back down, and smiled.

Chapter Fourteen

The End, The Beginning,
The Beautiful Thing We Do

Sprawled on the attic floor, amidst scattered sheets of paper, I awoke the next morning with my face stuck to the last page in Granddad's story. My hand was still gripped tightly around the pen I'd used to write the final chapter. It was done. I'd finished my project for Mr. Weiss. If this didn't convince him of the importance of one single mouse, then nothing would. I wiped my wet cheek on my sleeve, gathered the pages, and headed toward my room to get ready for school.

Before I could even enter the Ward Middle double doors, cheers of support rang in my ears.

"Wow," said Kristen when I entered homeroom. "I knew we would get advocates, but this is amazing! The whole school is behind you. Did you finish the paper? Is it good? I mean, of course it is! I know it's awesome. Are you nervous?"

"I'm fine." A wide, confident grin spread across my face. I couldn't help but find Kristen's assumption that I was nervous comical. I knew what magic I had in store for Mr. Weiss, but no one else did, at least not yet.

Fifth period took longer to arrive that day than it had any day prior. For the first time ever, I actually welcomed Mr. Aslo's first period Math class because I knew it meant I was one hour closer to my moment. After what felt like a century – no, I'm exaggerating, after what felt like half a century – the lunch bell finally brought me some reprieve.

"Would you like more gravy?" asked the sweet grey-haired lunch lady who always gave me the most generous of helpings even when I hadn't asked for them.

"No ma'am, but thank you." Kristen was beside me getting her tray filled with plain rice while trying to convince the sweet grey-haired lunch lady that brown rice should be served in its place.

"Doesn't it seem like we have rice and gravy as a side every day?" she whispered as we made our way through the line.

"Yeah, now that you mention it."

"So, you have to tell me about what you wrote," she demanded while prodding me through the line.

"Well, it's not just what *I* wrote," I replied with a satisfied smile.

"What do you mean?"

"I used my granddad's story."

"Wait, what? But you were supposed to write something yourself."

"Oh I did. You'll see. The pages stopped last night, and I wrote the final chapter myself. I finished my granddad's story."

Kristen tilted her head to scratch her eyebrow. I'd been her friend long enough to know that when she scratched her eyebrow, it always meant she wanted to ask a question.

"Yes?" I prodded and waited. I knew she wanted to read what I had written.

"Can I?" she asked.

"Here." I took the papers out of my backpack and pushed them across the table where we had settled with our starchy lunches. "Just make sure to give them back before the fifth period bells rings, okay?"

"Of course!" replied Kristen.

When the fifth period bell rang, Kristen was nowhere to be found. Everyone had already taken their seats. Mr. Weiss stood at the front of the classroom checking off each present student on the roll call list. When he saw Kristen's empty chair, he immediately looked at me as if I knew of her whereabouts. At that moment there was nothing I wanted to know more.

Where is she? In my head it sounded more like a cry than a thought, but I kept repeating the question over and over until I finally saw her running into the classroom.

"Ms. Emerson, you're late!" Mr. Weiss bellowed as if he'd accomplished a great feat by spotting her before she'd had a chance to blend in with her seated classmates. A little out of breath, Kristen stopped to tip her forefinger at Mr. Weiss and wink.

"Yes sir, I am, but the reason was worth being marked tardy," Kristen replied. She sat down in the desk behind me. "I sent your paper to the paper," she whispered in my ear.

"Wait, what?" But Kristen ignored my question and continued speaking to Mr. Weiss.

"Yes, sir, Mr. Weiss, it was worth it. You'll understand when you read this." Kristen sprang from her seat and delivered my stack of handwritten papers to Mr. Weiss. "This is my best friend's work, started by her grandfather and finished by her, and I think you'll find it to be more than satisfactory. I know the editor of Ward Middle News sure did, and…the editor of the State Times!"

Since that moment, my life has not been the same. Mr. Weiss read the story my grandfather and I had written together. It not only moved him to pardon the mice assigned to our class but to all future classes as well. The editor of the State Times emailed our story to his wife who just happened to be the head of a major publishing house. At her insistence, I wrote this book. I wrote the book that told *my* story.

Sometimes I'm still amazed by all of it. I'm still amazed by everything that did happen so that everything could happen. If you've ever experienced something coming together with such ease that it seemed every moment prior had been a guided tour on a tailor-made journey to bring you to that one special moment in time, then you know what I mean.

I am forever grateful for the love Granddad showed me in his story and for the gift he gave me in those blank pages. I imagine somewhere, somehow, there is a trunk for my granddad to visit. There is a trunk where he sits and reads every word I've written. There is a trunk where a small messenger delivers to him each night the pages of this story. After all, that's what we do, isn't it? Those who come before us begin a story, and we do our best to tell our part, picking up where they left off, delivering each page as we go. It's a beautiful thing we do. It's a beautiful thing to write your story.

The End